The Pontmercy's of Paris

The story of
Marius and Cosette
after the Death of
Jean Valjean.

W. James Read

Library of Congress Catalog Card Number: 96-92832
ISBN 1-57502-339-3

Additional copies are available.
For your convenience, an order form can
be found at the back of this book.

Cover Artwork by Melissa Remolde

Printed in the USA by

Morris
PUBLISHING

3212 E. Hwy 30
Kearney, NE 68847
800-650-7888

PREREQUISITE

Although remote, the possibility exists that you have not read "Les Misérables". If this is the case, please pursue the far superior original first.

DEDICATION

Dearest Kimberly,

Most probably, you and I will be the only ones interested enough to read this story. It is a humble attempt to continue the saga of "Les Misérables", a sequel, if you will. The tale that we both love, and hated to see end, extends into the future. The future of 19th century France that is.

I've studied that era and done some research, but, basically wanted the story to go on the way Victor Hugo would have wanted it to. Although we both have seen the rousing and splendid live musical performance at different times, perhaps we can enjoy it together (with our spouses of course) at some future date.

Many thanks to my daughter, Joanne, for the word processing part of this endeavor.

Love,

Dad-Val-Dad

THE PONTMERCY'S OF PARIS

FRANCINE

PIERRE

GRANDCHILDREN

Chapter I

MARIUS AND COSETTE

. . . .

BEGINNINGS

That plain, unmarked headstone was visited often during the first year of the marriage of Marius and Cosette Pontmercy. Under that stone were the physical remains of a man whose soul was surely with the angels. It was the humble grave of Jean Valjean. Yes, Jean Valjean, the guardian angel of Cosette and later, Marius, at the ill-fated barricade.

Marius on numerous occasions said to himself and also to Cosette, "I wish I had time to know him better, after the truth was finally uncovered. He always seemed so sad and mysterious and then to learn of his past as a convict, I had much mistrust and didn't care to see him all that often. If only we had a few more weeks, or even days, to talk and receive answers relative to the releasing of Javert and the barricade and the arduous trek through the sewers of Paris."

Cosette thought long and hard about Fantine, her mother, just a faint shadow from early childhood. "She had suffered much," Cosette mused to herself. "But in what way? And where was she living then?" The long and nightmarish years with the Thénardiers were also a distant memory. There seemed to be an invisible barrier implanted from the time the kindly gentleman lifted the pail of water in the woods and changed her life forever.

Of course, the change that mattered most to her now was the first time her eyes met those of beloved Marius. That led to romance and marriage to the man with whom she wanted to spend the rest of her life and be the father of her children. Cosette really had no other friends of the opposite sex. Those five or six years at the convent were spent catching up on an education, which found her over a year behind when she arrived.

It goes without saying there were no boys there and very little chance of meeting any. As she grew older, the controlled walks with Jean Valjean left virtually no opportunity to socialize. If it were not for the persistence of Marius, and the help given by Eponine, the courtship most certainly would not have been consummated. After the long convalescing period and the wedding and process of entering married life residing at Rue des Filles du Calvaire, No. 6, Marius began to grow restless.

He and Cosette began taking long walks during the spring and early summer months in 1833. They walked for hours during any given week. Marius would take out his law books for a while and if it was a nice day, by mid-morning his bride could easily be convinced they would enjoy the outdoors much more than being housebound. The pair walked in the city and in the country, usually stopping for a bit of lunch before returning home in the early afternoon. Conversation flowed freely between them and they traded future dreams and lofty expectations of life during these happy, carefree hours.

Marius occasionally walked alone and it was on one of these excursions that he encountered a commotion that roused him from his euphoric intoxication with life and love and sunshine blended with fresh spring air. Located in a poorer section of Paris he asked the nearest person, "Citizen, can you tell me something of this disturbance?" As a small, slightly emaciated wiry fellow in his thirties was led away handcuffed by a local constable, the reply was given, "Citizen Vinet at your service, Monsieur. Poor fellow was just arrested. Don't know his name, but from what I gather he had a very sick daughter who needed medical attention desperately. Problem was, he had no money and lacking the proper connections the doctor ignored him. He pleaded with the doctor for days with no avail. Finally the doctor, a much taller man, was accosted by the man who beat on the doctor's chest with his fists. Didn't hurt him much I'm sure but he still had the man arrested for assault. Now he'll spend a year or two in jail, you can bank on that."

As M. Vinet began to leave the area, Marius inquired, "What will happen to his daughter now?" The man paused briefly and answered, "The daughter Monsieur, died last night." "The doctor's name, Citizen?" "Oh, I think they said LaPointe or something similar."

Marius now sensed the time had arrived for him to pursue his law career and be out in the business world. The time for long walks, deep thoughts and endless speculation needed to be exchanged for deeds and activities necessary for his maturity and development in his current surroundings.

An older attorney, whom Marius had met the previous year at a dinner, was the one he sought out. Monsieur Nungusser had expressed interest in retiring in a few years and was looking for a young lawyer with whom he could share his practice and gradually turn over the reins of the business. Marius remembered liking his style and his reputation and hoped the gentleman had not yet found his junior partner.

Marius left at mid-morning on the brisk 20-minute walk that would take him the law office. Earlier, he and Cosette had a scrumptious breakfast and he was definitely feeling optimistic in regard to visiting Nungusser. He even mused to himself that as much as he was enjoying this walk he would almost certainly utilize a fiacre in times of inclement weather or severe cold.

Upon reaching the door, Marius encountered a middle-aged woman. "Is Monsieur Nungusser available?" he inquired. "That depends. Do you have an appointment?" she said. "Not exactly," returned Marius, "I'm an old acquaintance."

Just as Madame Secretary was about to continue her interrogation, M. Nungusser opened the door to his office and peered out. After a brief pause, Marius was relieved to hear him inquire "Monsieur Pontmercy, is that you?" "Yes," replied Marius, "so good of you to remember."

"Step into my office, Marius, and we'll talk for a while," offered Attorney Nungusser.

"Thank you," a somewhat relieved Marius replied. "I was hoping you could spare a few minutes. I do have an important matter to discuss this morning. Could you be so kind as to tell me if you've hired an associate yet?"

"Why yes I did," he said as he stroked his chin, "about two months ago." Marius' heart sank as he gazed around the room at the myriad of volumes that were available in the office. "But he didn't work out. Lasted less than a month. Just wasn't ambitious or energetic enough."

Marius hopefully inquired "I assume you're looking for a replacement?" The elder lawyer, now quite certain of Marius' intentions, replied "That is correct. Are you interested in some hard but challenging work?"

"Indeed I am," said Marius, "When could I start?" "I need you here next Monday, Marius. In the meantime, take this folio home and read it over carefully. You will have new responsibilities and I want you to know what will be expected of you. We can discuss your questions and compensation Monday morning."

"Thank you ever so much," declared Marius as he rose from his chair, "I'll try not to disappoint you." Marius left the building and walked home with a new spring in his step.

Nicolette greeted Marius on his arrival home. "Were you successful on your interview?", already sensing that he was. "It certainly went well. I'll be starting on Monday and it will be good to make myself useful again."

He hurried inside and found Cosette. Taking care to walk up quietly behind her, he gave her a gigantic hug and exclaimed "I'm now among the employed of Paris." "That's wonderful, dearest. I'm sure you'll do well and give it your best." "I will, you can count on that." "Lunch is ready, I guess you're hungry after your big morning. Oh, by the way, I have some disturbing news to tell you. The doctor is sending Basque to a sanitarium. He may have pneumonia or worse. I wish he would have gone for treatment sooner."

IS THE FIRST CASE HOPELESS?

Marius, true to his word, did give his all to his new position in the law office. The first months were spent learning all he could from his experienced mentor. He learned quickly, so he was told. M. Nungusser knew a promising young prospect when he saw one and did not hold back anything in the educational process. He liked the way Marius applied himself and usually spent an extra hour per day at the office, over and above what was expected in his contract.

The time came when Marius could be assigned to a case as the primary counsel, with his mentor on the sidelines for advice and assistance. The case designated was the defense of a barricade survivor. Those revolutionaries not killed in the fighting who were taken prisoner were held pending trials. Some of the wounded were among the last to be tried and Marius was to defend one of the last of those. He was a very bitter man, disliked by all and he disliked and mistrusted most others in return. The prisoner's name was Jacques Bauchet.

Standing well over six feet tall and weighing in excess of 220 pounds, Jacques had been shot in the back in the vicinity of the barricades the previous summer. Although the wound hit no vital organs and was not life threatening, there was a hideous elongated scar on the right side of his back. The surgeon had a difficult time locating the projectile and was not nearly as gentle as he might have been, had the victim been a model citizen and not a revolutionary.

The charges against Bauchet carried a 20 year prison term and, as he was only 32 years of age, the state was anticipating a score of years at hard labor from the fully recovered prisoner. The case against him seemed to be air tight, and Jacques saw no reason for the least bit of optimism. His counsel shared the lack of hope that was apparent.

Marius entered the room used for interviewing defendants and recesses in the court proceedings. He quickly glanced around the room, which contained a long rectangular table and about a dozen chairs, and said to the prisoner, "M. Bauchet, I'm your court appointed counsel, Marius Pontmercy."

Obviously unimpressed, the prisoner continued staring at the table top and mumbled "You're wasting your time." "Oh, how is that? You are entitled to legal counsel and advice," Marius added. The prisoner now looked up for the first time and eyed Marius, who was seated across the table from him, "I said, you're wasting your time. They have me for twenty years. I have a record. I would've been executed, except I was wounded. They probably should have finished it right then."

"But, they didn't and now you have a chance. I know what it means to have a slim chance for life."

"Sure you do, Monsieur Lawyer, you know nothing about the risks I've taken in my life recently."

"Someday maybe I'll tell you," Marius continued. "Now Jacques, what were you doing down by the barricades? Were you firing at the National Guard?"

"No. Not that it matters. There was heavy fighting and I made my way behind rebel lines. It was still very dark, but I knew several soldiers were down from their wounds." The prisoner hesitated.

"Go on." Marius said. "I want to hear everything."

"Alright, I'll go on. Twice before, I had pulled wounded officers to safety and medical attention. I was rewarded quite well by a Lieutenant, more money than I could earn in a month at least. I was not on one side or the other in this dispute, just trying to earn my living."

"You sound sincere, Jacques, but tell me, How did you acquire your prior criminal record?"

"I am sincere, Monsieur. I have no family. I was raised by the state as an orphan. By desertion while still an infant, I'm told. After the lower grades at the state school, I learned some carpentry and became something of a handyman. In my early twenties I traveled around the country doing odd jobs for short periods of time. I put down no roots. I worked in Southern France during winter and swung up north when the warmer months arrived.

When I was 25, I remodeled some rooms for a wealthy business man who had a large estate. He kept adding items to be done, far more than our original agreement. Six weeks of work turned into three months. I was patient for a while but soon was running out of money. I did get to know the layout of his home real well, though. I knew where he kept his money and valuables. I stopped protesting to the man and bided my time until the job was finally completed to his satisfaction. That last afternoon when I applied the finishing touches, no one was home except for two servants. When the man, who seemed to serve as a butler-gardener, was outside tending the flowers and the middle-aged lady who cooked and cleaned was occupied, I decided to make my move. I took money from a bureau drawer, no more than I truly deserved, and a jeweled bracelet that caught my eye. That bracelet turned out to be a mistake as it lead to my arrest, ten days later. The money may not have been missed for a long time, but the bracelet was missed and reported. I was caught and spent 5 years in prison, and now you know my story, such as it is."

"Very interesting, to say the least, Jacques. My job will be to convince the court that you are telling the truth and save you from 20 years of hell, which, in all probability, would be a "life" sentence for you, considering your age."

"Do you think I have any chance at all, Monsieur?"

"You have two chances. Slim and none! We shall try to make it the former. In the meantime, Jacques, keep yourself clean shaven, sit and stand erect, look people in the eye when they speak to you. You're a citizen of France, with nothing to lose by having a positive attitude. Who knows, with God's help, you may have a chance to gain your freedom. And don't forget to tell me any details you may have forgotten today, when we have our next meeting."

Marius was gathering his notes when the guards arrived to take the prisoner back to his cell. He noticed that Jacques was no longer looking down at the table top, but his gaze met that of the guards. Even though they jostled him along just as roughly as before, he didn't seem to mind the rough treatment as much."

The following morning at the breakfast table, Cosette was the first to speak. "You were up very late last night, dearest. Will Paris' newest attorney do this often and neglect his loving wife?" she asked with one of her impishly precious smiles.

"I would not neglect you, if I were working on a dozen cases, my love," Marius replied. "However, this is my first real case and it's quite intriguing." "More intriguing than I am?" The debate continued. "Of course not, you're always at the top of my priority list, my dear."

"Oh, is that so?" Cosette prodded.

"You know, you weren't so captivating the first time I saw you, my lark. I was much more intrigued with your guardian in those days."

"Tell me more, husband."

"Well, since you asked, my colleagues and I who walked in that park were very curious as to whether he was a retired military veteran or not. Also, what was his relationship to you, grand-father, uncle, father? We discussed that often."

"Your friends and you were wrong on all counts."

"I suppose we were, but at least it generated some conver-sation. And the best was yet to come. After a six month absence I returned to find you had changed. What an awesome improve-ment in a very short time."

"Better than any six month period in your life, dearest?"

"You can be sure of that, my love. Could I have more coffee?" Marius added, hoping to escape the present conversation.

As Cosette poured, she managed to get in the last word by adding, "I was very young when you first saw me, but when you fell, you fell hard. Probably harder than I'll ever know. Do you still love me?"

"What do you think?" Marius replied, and ignoring his coffee began chasing Cosette in the direction of their sleeping quarters amid squeals of delight. Love was certainly grand for this couple.

A week later Jacques Bauchet received some disturbing news. News acquired through the prison grapevine, so to speak. Another barricade trial had ended with a guilty verdict. The sen-tence was usually very predictable, prescribing fifteen or twenty years at hard labor, or occasionally an execution by firing squad. Either prospect seemed grim and depressing to Jacques. However, he had one thing to buoy his hopes since the recent visit with counsel. He had vowed to take care of himself and keep an optimistic attitude. Other prisoners, even the younger ones, seemed to give in to despair. They were unkempt, slouching and argumentative and did nothing to impress their captors. This was not going to happen to him. Not anymore. His spirit would never again be broken, at least not until after his trial verdict was given. He did have one ally in the person of his counsel, Jacques thought to himself. Monsieur Pontmercy, brand new attorney, seems to be a likeable fellow and will probably try very hard to win his first case. I hope he doesn't try too hard and lose it all. Poor fellow, he probably wouldn't recognize a barricade if he tripped over one.

The physical condition of Basque was not improving and word from the sanitorium that reached No. 6 Rue des Filles indicated he never would recover. Marius had a replacement in mind, in the person of Marcel Ylonen. A likeable middle-aged man he was acquainted with from the law office and the court house. Marcel was interested in transferring his talents to domestic services when a suitable opportunity presented itself. He received an offer he felt impossible to refuse so it was readily accepted.

Marius looked up from his desk as M. Nungusser offered some information. "Here's the trial notice for J. Bauchet. Commencing next week, I see. What's your feeling about this man?" "Innocent of these particular charges, at least," Marius answered. "No witnesses on his behalf however."

"Don't overlook anything," his mentor continued. "The prosecutors are used to easy victories, especially in these current times. A small truth well presented may mean a lot."

"I'll keep that in mind and, thanks for your help regarding this case. Oh, I'll be visiting Jacques this afternoon."

It was immediately apparent to Marius that Jacques had taken the advice, relative to his appearance. He no longer looked like a guilty ax-convict, but rather a carpenter in fresh work clothes.

"Good afternoon," Marius said. "You look much better than the first time we met." "Good afternoon counselor. I'm trying to make a good impression here. I seem to be getting more respect from the other prisoners, at least. One inmate even asked me for advice about his pending trial." "That's good, Jacques, keep it up and try not to be discouraged. Your trial's scheduled for next week. I think well make a good showing."

"I hope so, Monsieur. I don't want to spend the rest of my life in prison."

"Nor do I want to see you there. I believe everything you've told me and soon I must convince others to embrace similar feelings. By the way, Jacques, do you remember the surgeon's name who operated on your wound? I may want to put him on the stand."

"That's a name I never forgot M. Pontmercy. Not with a scar like mine, it's easy to remember. Dr. Labrecque it is. One of his assistants asked him to slow down and do a neater job on the incision and stitches. He didn't care, though. Just another doomed prisoner to him."

"I'm sure you're not the only one treated that way, Jacques. He probably has no conscience. Someday he will be held accountable for his carelessness. I must leave now, but I'll see you next Monday, about an hour before the trial begins." "Until then counselor."

Over the weekend Marius seemed quiet and withdrawn to his wife, who asked him, "This case means so much to you dear, are you nervous about getting started?" "A little bit, of course, I'm trying to envision all possible directions the testimony may lead." "Will your employer be present during the proceedings?"

"He will be there in the first row behind the participants. We will confer during any recesses or other breaks, such as meals and the like."

"Try to relax and enjoy yourself the rest of the weekend. I'm sure you'll do better if you're well rested and fresh for the new week."

"Cosette, my love, you're right of course. I know I'm well prepared and my mentor will be close at hand. It's just difficult to think about Jacques' future, should I fail."

"Well, try to remember dear, I'll be thinking of you often this week and praying that all goes well for your client and you."

"I'm really a fortunate man, having an angel like you to come home to. I know that however the case is decided, your love and support will remain unchanged."

THE TRIAL

By the time the sun first emerged on the distant horizon, Jacques Bauchet had been awake for well over an hour. In fact, he hadn't slept very much at all with the trial and all it's ramifications weighing heavily on his mind. He hardly touched his breakfast and just sat thoughtfully as he awaited the arrival of his defense counsel.

True to his word, Marius walked into the holding area approximately an hour before the proceedings were scheduled to commence. "Hello Jacques. Are you ready for a difficult day?" "Good morning Monsieur, and I guess I'm as ready as I'll ever be."

"Jacques, the plan of action I'm taking is basically set. All I want you to do, is to tell the truth in every respect if you are called to the stand. I think your presentable appearance and your positive attitude will surprise many in the courtroom. However, the main reason I wanted to talk to you this morning so early was something totally different. The first time we met I told you that I, once, had only a slim chance for survival. You undoubtedly think I've led a sheltered life, studied and became a lawyer. Not always so. In fact, although you may find this hard to believe, I was actively involved at the barricade of the Rue de la Chanvrerie, joining a number of my friends. During the barricades fall, amid furious fighting, I was severely wounded with bullet and bayonet and fell near death. I was single, of course at the time, but my wife's guardian, who had infiltrated the barricade, gathered me up and lacking any other avenue of escape, carried me for over a mile through the sewers of Paris. Needless to say, I survived and am now at your service."

Jacques was completely astonished by the revelation he had just heard. "I had no idea," M. Pontmercy. "Although I appreciated your appointment as my defense counselor, it never dawned on me that true adversity was a part of your life. It seems I've completely misjudged you."

"I see the time has come, Jacques" Marius said as two gendarmes arrived to escort his client into the courtroom. When Marius entered the large room he observed it to be fairly well packed with spectators along with all the required participants. He acknowledged M. Nungusser with a short handshake as he walked by to join his client.

A tall well dressed man with a confident air about him caught Jacques attention and he asked, "Who is that, Monsieur?" "That's our main adversary, prosecuting attorney Rene Duquette. A man not accustomed to losing, especially in these barricade cases, I've been told."

"Now I am worried, Monsieur." "Well Jacques, he's only human, and he hasn't seen the likes of us yet." The defendant wasn't sure exactly what that last statement meant, so he remained silent.

When all the parties concerned were seated in their proper places, prosecutor Duquette began his searing indictment. "You see before you Jacques Bauchet, enemy of the state. Former convict, served five years for robbery and, most recently, while aiding a student insurrection was wounded and captured at a barricade. That's right, shot in the act, with a squad of guardsmen as witnesses. He's guilty as sin, no doubt about it."

After the squad leader testified in agreement to prosecutors statement, Marius had only one question for him, "Was the defendant armed when he was captured, Monsieur?" "He could have thrown his weapon aside" came the reply. "Just a yes or no answer, if you please." "No," was the one word answer.

Rene Duquette sat with a confident sneer etched on his face. To his right was the squad leader of the National Guard and the row behind him contained many members of the group who either chose to be there, or perhaps were ordered to be present. He declined to put anyone else on the stand, expecting a speedy verdict and also expecting to be punctual for a luncheon meeting with a business associate to discuss an investment. He had the assurance of his right to cross-examine, should the defense present any surprise witnesses.

A man had entered the chamber shortly after the defendant and his counsel took their places. He was not there of his own accord, but rather acquiescing to a subpoena recently received. Marius, surmising that he must be present, rose to continue to present his case for the defense.

"Dr. Serge Labrecque to the stand," called the clerk in his slightly nasally monotone voice. As he strode forward, the counsel for the defense quickly assessed the surgeon, who although his testimony should be beneficial to his client, owed much of his livelihood to the military, and thus his loyalties.

"Tell the court, Dr. Labrecque, are you the surgeon who operated on the defendant and eventually removed the projectile?" "Yes I am," the doctor answered, "and why did you say eventually? I resent that remark." "My client told me he was in surgery a long time, with very little anesthesia. Should we show the court and yourself the resulting scar?"

"That will not be necessary," was the curt reply.

"Tell us also, Doctor, have you performed surgery on a great many other combatants, both the military and the rebels as well?" "That's correct, dozens of times."

"And isn't it true," Marius continued, "that you reserve your best work for the police and the military?"

"Objection!" roared Duquette in protest.

"The question is withdrawn," Marius said amid no small murmuring from the audience and a smile from M. Nungusser.

"Well then, doctor, I assume you treat wounds to the head and chest wounds and arms and legs also," he said, pointing to the corresponding parts of his own body as he spoke.

"Yes, of course."

"Would you agree, doctor, that the vast majority of the injuries you treat are to the anterior or frontal part of the body?"

The doctor, somewhat on the defensive by this point, answered "Certainly that's true. Probably ninety percent or better are anterior shots."

"Where was the defendant shot, doctor?"

"The defendant was shot in the back."

"And the projectile was standard military issue?"

"Yes, it was."

"No further questions, doctor."

The judge inquired of prosecutor Duquette, "Do you wish to cross examine?" "No, that should not be necessary," was the reply. A brief fifteen minute recess was announced by Judge Rochefort.

During the break, M. Nungusser seemed optimistic with the proceedings thus far. He reminded Marius, "The decision could go either way. Remember, you must be very convincing with your closing remarks." "I know. I'll try to appeal to their sense of fairness. The opposition doesn't seem quite as smug as they were earlier in the morning."

"Will I be put on the stand, Counselor?" Jacques asked. "No, I don't think so. The possible cross examination may do more harm than good. I'll tell the jury your story and hopefully they'll accept it." The reconvening was then announced by the clerk.

With the absence of more witnesses, the Judge asked Marius to give his remarks to the jury. He began the most important minutes of his fledgling career.

"The defendant, Jacques Bauchet, has had a tough life growing up as an orphan here in Paris. He made a mistake and paid for it dearly, spending five years in prison. Upon his release within the last two years, employment has been next to impossible for someone carrying a yellow card. When fighting erupted in the city, Jacques discovered a new way to earn some money. A very risky way to say the least. He rescued a wounded and dying officer and was rewarded for his actions after that person received medical treatment. He was performing the same service for somebody the morning he was shot. Gentlemen of the jury, the defendant was not shot in the chest as he would have been, if he was associated with the revolutionaries, facing and firing at the military. No, he was shot in the back as he was moving the wounded officer toward the militaries lines. The defendant is not guilty of the charge against him."

The jury began its deliberations and neither M. Duquette nor the defense team left the room. The former because he still expected a prompt guilty verdict and the latter due to their cautious hopefulness. A portion of the general public departed, due in part to their approaching noonday meal. An hour passed and the prosecuting attorney began to grow restless and glanced several times at his timepiece. As the time of deliberation drew nearer to the end of the second hour the door opened and the court was reconvened.

Judge Rochefort asked the jury foreman, "Have you reached a verdict?"

"We have, your honor."

"And how do you find?"

"Not guilty, your honor."

After the clamor of response in the hall had subsided to a degree, Rene Duquette stood up abruptly. Knocking his chair over backwards in the process he said for anyone interested enough to listen "The fools" and stormed out of the building.

That clamor of response, almost entirely favorable with the verdict, prompted a brief embrace between Marius and Jacques. They were joined by M. Nungusser, who said "You're a free man Jacques and I don't think a job will be too hard to find in the area now. And, congratulations are in order for you, Marius my boy."

THE FUTURE IS FORMING

Naturally Marius was on top of the world for quite some time after the trial. Even so, his mentor was not slow to remind him that there was much to be learned and long hours of work and research to be endured. M. Nungusser planned to work another year or two, and then Marius would be completely on his own.

Life in general at the Gillenormand house was dramatically revitalized with the addition of Cosette and Marius some months ago after their wedding. By this time Marius knew he was heir to the property, with the understanding that Mlle. Gillenormand would always have a place to live and her needs met.

After Marius had been employed at the law office for nine or ten months, Cosette approached him with this question "Dearest, I need to find a useful outlet for some of my energy while you're at work." "I guess I can see your point, my dear. With Nicolette and Marcel available for most of the chores, it could be somewhat boring, waiting for me to get home." "Try to be serious now," Cosette continued. "I've been thinking of doing some volunteer work. Most probably at Paris General Hospital, where the work would be appreciated and needed."

"Now that sounds like a wonderful idea. I'm sure you'd brighten that place like a burst of sunlight." "I'd love to be stationed in the children's ward unless there is a more urgent need for help in another area." "How many hours are you planning to spend there?" "Probably four to six hours a day, and perhaps one or two days a week. I'll see how it goes."

"Sounds like an ambitious goal, my dear. I suppose you'll try to begin as soon as possible?"

"I'm hoping to start next week, if everything works out well."

"Cosette, my darling, they'd be very foolish not to add an angel to their staff, in a place that's no stranger to pain and suffering."

The hospital was not slack in bolstering their volunteer work force with a heavenly body. And the children, long used to upper middle aged attendants, were uplifted in their convalescence by this newcomer who moved about like a butterfly in a field of flowers. So Cosette spread her love to those most in need, and enjoyed herself immensely in the process.

These were happy days for the Pontmercy's. A time of growing together and blending in with their community and their work places. Sometime during late fall in 1834, Cosette who was spreading so much love both at home and in the hospital, herself was the beneficiary of a seed of love implanted within her own being.

Marriage is honourable in all, and the bed undefiled: but whoremongers and adulterers God will judge.

Heb. 13:4

Chapter II

JEAN AND EPONINE

. . . .

Early in the year, which was 1835, Cosette had something important to relate to Marius. Important, happy and wonderful news to be sure. She was expecting. Expecting what you might ask. A new wardrobe, a visit from royalty, a promotion for Marius. No, none of those — she was expecting the birth of a child. Probably around mid-summer a new member would be added, making theirs a true family in every sense of the word.

Marius, upon arriving home from work, asked "Why are you in such a splendid mood today, my precious?" "Why don't you try to guess, Dear" said Cosette.

"I have no idea, really."

"Well I'm not going to tell you if you don't try."

"I'm at a loss, may I have a clue or two?"

"Only one clue — and it's a large one. Have you noticed I'm a little nauseous sometimes in the morning?"

"Why yes — that's right. Oh Cosette, does this mean what I think it does, my love?"

"It does."

"It does? Are you sure?"

"I'm sure."

"Will we have a son?"

"I'm not sure about that, Marius."

"Well that's alright. This is wonderful news. Boy or girl, the child must be healthy, that's the most important thing. We are heaven blessed my princess."

The following morning the entire household learned about the pregnancy. M. Gillenormand commented, "It's about time I became a legitimate great-grandfather."

Even though the blessed event was some months away, it was obvious things were changing for the happy pair. Their two year 'honeymoon' had come to an end and they began thinking and planning as parents. The guest room next to their bedroom would become the nursery. Shopping for furniture, the necessary crib and cradle and the like would begin when spring arrived. Ah, spring. The expecting parents had every reason to believe it would be a delightful spring and a very blessed summer to follow.

THE NAME GAME

After a relatively uneventful winter, spring did arrive in all it's glory. Marcel had the grounds in wonderful condition with new-blooming flowers everywhere. Warm days and plenty of rainfall combined to make natures job easy in Paris that year. Attorney Marius enjoyed his work and found it both challenging and, at times, very rewarding. Cosette was enjoying herself and looking forward to her future motherhood. By that time, she had left her weekly role as a volunteer worker at the hospital, although she vowed to return after the child was, perhaps two years old.

Sometime in late April or early May, the pair began to think seriously about names for the first time. "What will we name the baby?" asked Cosette as she customarily began the discussion.

"Why don't you tell me the sex of the baby?" Marius countered.

"I don't know, silly."

"That's not a silly question, dearest. It would make the task of choosing a name much simpler."

"Well, my helpful husband, I'll pick a girl's name and you can choose a boy's name. How does that sound?"

"That's a poor idea. We should both agree on a name regard-less of the baby's sex. Let's be fair about this."

"You mean you're not going to insist on having a 'little Marius' around the house? I'm truly surprised."

"Of course not. Maybe George, after my father."

"Now that's out of the question. How about Jean, to honor the man who saved your life and probably mine as well."

"It looks like we've finally agreed on something, dearest. I have every reason to like that name."

"That settles it then. It will probably be a boy anyway, my dear husband."

"Don't forget, it could be a girl and now I will choose our daughters name. The name of someone else who performed a great deed for us."

"Now who could that be?"

"Eponine."

"Eponine?"

"That's right. The one who shielded me from a bullet at the barricade should get some respect as well."

"I never liked that name or that family either. They were a pack of scoundrels, Marius."

"Please don't feel that way. This will be a new Eponine who will grow up with our love."

"I don't know. Are there any other choices?"

"Not really. Without her help, and her sacrifice, we wouldn't be together now. You know I'm right about this."

"Well, I guess it's settled then."

"Great, they're perfect choices. Can I have one of your patented smiles now?"

Cosette tried to say no, but she was already grinning from ear to ear. They were now prepared for a son or a daughter or even fraternal twins.

Spring soon led into summer. Cosette was enjoying a problem-free pregnancy and looking forward to ushering in a new arrival to the family. By mid July the area was locked in a brutal heat wave. The high humidity along with temperatures continually in the nineties was taking a toll on Cosette, as she entered the final month of her pregnancy. In early August the heat wave, at last, subsided.

It was Saturday morning and quite pleasant when Marius shared an idea with his wife. "You really need to get out and enjoy some fresh air, my dear. I'll get the carriage ready and we'll take some food and take a short ride in the country."

"I'd like that, but will that carriage ride be too rough and bouncy for me? I'm only two or three weeks away from delivering, you know."

"We'll take it real easy. I'll drive so slow the turtles will pass us, Marius joked."

"Be serious now, husband. I don't want to travel more than a few miles."

"That's a promise. I'll have you back home by early afternoon." The couple soon departed and, although they weren't passed by any turtles, they were overtaken by just about everything else in motion. A pleasant area was observed less than two miles outside of the city and they spread out the light blanket which was taken along. After they finished lunch Marius said, "This is a great location here, I think I'm going to stretch out and take a short nap." "I hope it is short, dear, it is clouding up somewhat over to the west. " Within the next twenty minutes the gentle breeze had become a definite wind of some strength. Cosette noticed a strange twinge of pain in her abdomen and decided to rouse Marius. "Time to get up, dear, you can always sleep at home, if you must."

"As you wish, my love," he answered and began walking toward the horse and carriage. Just then a strong gust of wind snapped a large limb from a nearby tree. The limb crashed to the ground with a loud noise and the startled horse took off at a gallop.

When Cosette experienced a more severe pain she decided to advise Marius. "This is all new to me, but I think the baby's on the way soon."

"What? That's impossible — Isn't it?"

"I don't think it's impossible, considering how I feel right now." A rumble of thunder in the distance temporarily interrupted their conversation.

"Marius, we must return home as quickly as possible." "Agreed, but the horse is no longer in the area." "Just think of something - Oh, the pain is worse than before." Another clap of thunder resounded and this time much closer. A few drops of rain began to fall on the unfortunate pair. Marius helped Cosette over to the carriage, bringing the blanket with him. "You must stay here for now, dearest. I've got to locate that horse." "Please hurry, the pains are more regular now and more severe."

Marius ran in the direction the horse had taken earlier, but he was nowhere in sight. The rain intensified as he returned to the carriage. Cosette had some disturbing new for him. "I'm definitely in labor. This baby will be born in the rain and not in our own home, unless that horse comes back soon." "He's nowhere in sight and I haven't seen another soul anywhere."

Without revealing all the details, an hour later found Marius pulling the carriage himself, with the absence of the horse. In the carriage, Cosette held tightly to her new son, with a very soggy blanket covering all of the baby and barely half of herself. The whole ordeal had consumed just over two hours. Luckily for Marius, he had travelled only about 100 yards down the road when a fiacre approached heading into the city. Not counting the driver it was empty and able to accommodate the very wet group of travellers. Within twenty minutes they reached Paris General Hospital and proper medical attention. Marius, although soaked and exhausted, was thrilled with the news that mother and baby were doing just fine. He would never have forgiven himself if anything happened to either of them on this particular afternoon.

THE CHANGING OF THE GUARD

When Jean Pontmercy arrived home with his mother a few days later, it was obvious the infant now commanded the spotlight in that household. For nearly two years that privilege was, of course, reserved for the proud parents. Now they were happily sharing the bulk of the attention with their first born.

Marcels wife, Marie, with plenty of spare time on her hands, visited often and managed to find a way to help with the cooking or other chores, in order to spend time around the baby.

M. Gillenormand tried to show some enthusiasm for the new arrival but it was evident to all that his strength was waning rapidly. His vital organs that had served him well for over ninety years were wearing out, and there was no way of denying father time. Even the infants crying during the night tended to disturb his shallow sleep from several rooms down the hall.

Thus, after only two weeks from the infants arrival, the elderly gentleman slipped into his eternal reward during the night. Although his passing came as unexpectedly as it did, it was not a great shock for the household. Mlle. Gillenormand took it the hardest. She had become the senior member of the family and didn't like the inevitable being thrust upon her.

After the funeral, Marius said to Cosette and the others in the house, "I've never seen so many elderly people at the same time." "That's true," Cosette added, "It seemed like everyone over seventy years of age, that he ever knew attended the services." "He really had no younger friends," Nicolette contributed, "And in reality, most of his closest friends have passed away or the crowd would have been much larger." "It's hard to believe, but he was in his prime during the eighteenth century," Marius said. "That's long before most of us were born," a younger member of the group whispered.

Mlle. Gillenormand stayed in her room for the better part of a week, coming out only for a sparse meal or for the other necessities of life. She eventually terminated her period of mourning and actually became a more pleasant member of the household. Most living there thought she realized the majority of her life had passed her by and she needed to initiate some changes in order to find a source of enjoyment in the years which remained at her disposal.

ONE STEP FORWARD AND TWO BACK

The months rolled by quickly at the Pontmercy's home. Jean was healthy and growing and crawling around the rooms with a fair amount of speed. Then one day as Marius arrived home from work, he was greeted by his wife so enthusiastically, that he was almost bowled over. "Hurry inside dear, Jean can walk!" "Walk? He hasn't taken his first step yet, darling." "Well, he did today." "How many steps did he take?", Marius asked as he studied his crawling son. "Only one step," Cosette conceded, "But that's a start." "Of course it is, my dear," said Marius, trying not to dampen his wife's happiness.

Before the end of the month, Jean took those first steps and then soon linked a dozen together as he crossed the room from mother to father. His new found method to expend energy, tired the small boy and he slept soundly throughout the night. Then, one night, his sleep was broken by a dry nagging cough.

A few days later, at the breakfast table, Cosette shared this information, "Jean hasn't slept well lately, he's developed a persistent night cough." "I heard him once or twice, dear, but then I sleep more soundly than you do." "Mothers are light sleepers. I was with him for half the last two nights." "Perhaps he should see the doctor, what do you think?" "I had the same thought. He's definitely not himself in the daytime either."

Jean was worse than the day before, often the coughing fits lead to vomiting. Later that afternoon, Cosette's worst fears were realized as the doctor explained, "Your son is in the early stages of whooping cough. You may take him home now, but your house will be under quarantine for visitors, especially children. Give him this medication and keep me informed on his condition. I want to know immediately if convulsions occur. He must be hospitalized at that time."

Cosette, fighting back tears, answered "Yes doctor. Is there anything else I can do for him?" "We want to avoid dehydration. Give him plenty of liquids, provided he is keeping it down." "Of course, doctor, and I'll send word about his condition, or bring him if I have to."

When she arrived home, Cosette told Marcel to put a quarantine sign on the door. She also had this request, "Tell Marie to stay home until this illness is over. I'll get by with Nicolette's help." By the time Marius got home, she was rocking her wheezing son, with tears trickling down both cheeks.

Marius moved rapidly into the house after scanning the quarantine sign. "I see it's much worse than we thought, darling." After Cosette described the visit with the doctor, she added "We both must pray earnestly tonight that the Lord will see fit to spare our son from the worst of this dreadful disease. This can lead to brain damage or even death. Oh Marius, I love him so. I can't imagine life without him. I know I couldn't survive — and I don't think you could either."

"You must not have such morbid thoughts, darling. Jean will receive the best medical attention available in the city of Paris. He will recover, you'll see." "I wish that I had your optimism. You'll notice the difference in his cough the next time he starts. I can see why they named it as they did. It's horrible."

The baby seemed to hold his own, over the next two days. Was the medication helping? They didn't know for sure. The following day, Jean took a turn for the worse. His coughs ended with a 'whoop' and a clear sticky mucus was expelled. Once the baby shook violently after a coughing spell and Cosette, thinking it was a convulsion, had seen enough and they were off to the hospital. Doctor Bordet soon met them there and was of the opinion the baby should stay, convulsions or not. Marius, after notification by Marcel, left work early and joined his wife at the hospital. "I'm staying here tonight," Cosette announced, "It's all arranged. I don't want to leave him here without me, at least for the first night." "Whatever you think is best, dear. I assume it is permitted?" "Yes, I'll be here so he can see a familiar face and keep him calm. I must stay clear from the activities of the staff, though."

For the next few days, baby Jean suffered greatly with his coughing and periodic vomiting. It was indeed a monumental struggle to cling to life itself with such labored breathing. Cosette stayed with her son, sleeping only when he slept, suffering with him as he suffered. Marius visited after work for an hour or two, bringing with him clothes and other necessities required by his wife. For long periods of time they just sat together holding hands and looking at their son and at each other. Occasionally Cosette would say something impossible like 'Why can't one of us become ill and cough some and lessen the severity of the baby's illness'. And then Marius would just hold her hands a little tighter and say the words needed to comfort her and lessen her fears and give her the strength to carry on.

Doctor Bordet provided some encouragement by telling them it was good that their son was not fighting a high fever as well. He advised them also "The next couple of days are critical. He will most likely improve or his condition may worsen. In all likelihood he will not remain the same much longer." The couple just looked at him and nodded.

Jean again had a leveling off period in his condition and this time, much to the relief of his parents, he slowly began to improve rather than regressing, as he had done earlier. He remained in the hospital for ten more days before it was safe enough to be discharged. The crisis had passed and a lengthy period of convalescence in the home was underway.

It took a while, but he did return to complete health. The first month to get better and the next month to catch up to where the normal growing process would have taken him.

A GROWING FAMILY

By the time Jean was eighteen months old, and had enjoyed good health during the last four months, his mother once again was experiencing a familiar problem. Morning sickness. How do I tell Marius this time? She thought to herself. He may not be ready for another child yet. On the other hand, Jean will be over two years old when I deliver. He may be overjoyed with the news. But, on the other hand... And what about a name — if we have another boy? Oh, he can use his father's name, if he must. And if we have a girl, we have a name. Eponine, oh dear. I agreed to that name? He said I'd learn to love it. It will be a new Eponine.

Just then the front door opened and Marius was standing before her. "Oh, hello dear," was all the surprised Cosette could manage to say, with her recent thoughts weighing heavily on her mind.

"Is that the best greeting you have for your loving husband? Your husband who is home for the rest of the day, owing to a big snowstorm that has already begun." "Sorry dear, I haven't been out today and didn't notice the weather. Is all your work done at the office?" "All done, the timing is perfect. Actually we are in a slack period, with nothing pressing. I thought we could romp in the snow with Jean." "You two go ahead, I'm not in the mood for that today." A puzzled Marius went to help his son dress for outdoors.

Cosette pondered this new pregnancy on her own for several days before Marius finally pried from her the reason for her current malaise. Much to her relief, he was transported to a new height of euphoria, previously unknown to her.

"Of course I'm elated, dearest. I was a very lonely child growing up. I don't want Jean having the same experience. I'm not saying I want a dozen children but a daughter would certainly be wonderful, now that we have our son." "Well, I'm glad you feel that way. You never really told me how you felt about the size of our family." "Sorry dear, but I guess, now you know."

When early spring arrived, Marius received some news from M. Nungusser. "It appears the date of my retirement is now official. By the end of June you'll be on your own, Marius. More time has elapsed than I originally planned when you first came aboard, but now I've made my decision. Or should I say my wife made the decision for me. She wants very much to travel before we get too ancient to enjoy ourselves. Forty years is a long time to work and now I'm ready to take some leisure time."

"Congratulations are certainly in order" Marius replied, and I really appreciate the considerate way in which you shared your expertise in the practice of law." "That's quite all right, my boy. I knew almost immediately that you were the right choice for the position, not like that first flunkie I hired." "I enjoyed every minute and I hope you find time to visit the office whenever convenient in between your junkets." "Undoubtedly I will, and you must come and bring your wife to a dinner which will be given by my family in June." "I wouldn't miss it," Marius said, as their conversation turned to business.

Spring arrived and, it must be noted, was remarkably uneventful. As the career of Marius' mentor was winding down, the heir apparent was absorbing as much as humanly possible. He asked numerous questions, that he had not thought of earlier, and was growing in knowledge and confidence in the field of law.

A pleasant summer arrived, and this time there were no carriage rides in the country, even though the time of Cosette's delivery was still two months away. Early one evening in midsummer, a knock was heard at their front door.

Marius opened the door and encountered a tall, husky man. "Jacques Bauchet, it's been almost two years. How are you?" "Fine, M. Pontmercy." "Do come in, Jacques and meet my wife." "Thank you Monsieur." "You look well, Jacques. I take it you've found employment?" "Yes I have. After travelling and finding part-time work for a few months after my acquittal, I decided to return to this area and change my way of life. I've been employed by a cabinet maker for almost a year, and believe it or not, I'll be marrying this fall." "That's a remarkable change, Jacques," Cosette added to the conversation. "That's true, and I owe a great deal to your husband for his faith in me." "You don't owe me a thing, Jacques. Just keep up the good work. We may be looking you up for some furniture in the near future. As you can see we're expecting another child in the fall." "I'd be more than happy to take that order, Monsieur. But now, I must be on my way. We're making wedding plans, and someday I'd like to have a son myself, and teach him the skills of woodworking."

"Goodbye and good luck," the couple said to Jacques, almost in unison.

As the month of October made its entrance, the weather grew much stormier than remembered by many of the area residents. Several fierce gales blew in from the Atlantic, after having begun in a far distant place as tropical storms. One such gale advanced far inland, reaching the city of Paris.

It happened that Cosette, being annoyed by the banging of an out-building door that housed garden tools and the like, and seeing no sign of Marcel, decided to venture out and close it herself. After shutting the door securely, she began walking back to the house, when a small section of the end of the roof blew off in a mighty gust. The airborne section struck a hard blow to the back of her head and poor Cosette fell heavily to the ground.

The next thing the very pregnant and unfortunate dear remembered was waking up in the hospital with a blurry Marius and a nurse looking down at her. "What am I doing here?" she said slowly and with some difficulty. "Don't try to speak now, darling," her relieved husband told her. They tell me the baby is fine and you will be too, if you don't count a large headache." "This is awful, what hit me anyway?"

Marius related the details as best he knew them, after his briefing by Marcel. The latter was extremely upset, thinking his negligence with the shed door was responsible for the injury. In actuality it was, but Marius reminded him it was an accident and no permanent harm was done.

Before Cosette left the hospital, she gave birth to a baby girl on October 27, 1837. Without knowing it at the time, the Pontmercy's family was complete. Jean and Eponine were two children who would be raised in a loving family and be much adored. They, in turn, grew up to love and respect their parents, each other, and their neighbors around them.

And Cosette, being true to a promise made several years earlier, did return to her volunteer work at the hospital. In 1840, with ample help at home caring for her children, she felt compelled to return and care for other children less fortunate than her own.

But Jesus said, suffer little children and forbid them not, to come unto me: for of such is the kingdom of heaven.

Matt. 19:14

Chapter III

KIDNAPPED

• •

Ursula Drolet endured a brutal childhood. Eldest of five children, she became accustomed to hard work by the age of ten. Care for her three brothers and a single sister was thrust upon Ursula at her mother's earliest convenience. Failure to comply with her parents frequent orders met with swift reprisals in the form of beatings with the nearest non-lethal objects.

As she grew and matured, dreams of leaving home were constantly on her mind. Her development saw her become a huskier, slightly taller version of her mother. Strong body, basically homely appearance and limited academic intelligence was her lot. However, in scheming and conniving and general street awareness, Ursula ranked up near the top.

Her burning desire to depart from the domestic captivity that was so embittering, pushed the young woman into a major mistake in marrying Claude Tussaud. Claude was also a product of his environment. His father got drunk twice a month, the son every week. The father worked as little as possible, the son worked less, all he had to attract a wife was a run-down house inherited from an uncle on his father's side. At least the taxes were low.

It was to pay those taxes and to put bread on the table that found Madame Tussaud seeking employment as a cleaning woman at Paris General Hospital. Claude earned only slightly more than his drinking money as a journeyman Blacksmith and delivery man. The wages earned were more often in sous than francs. And so, the opportunistic Madame found work at the hospital just about half way in between the end of Cosette's first tour and the beginning of her second gratis association with the hospital.

A PLOT DEVELOPS

Unknown to her, Cosette acquired an enemy during her hours spent at the hospital as a nurse's aide. Madame Tussaud observed her from a distance and became obsessed with her beauty and her apparent affluence. She worked long and hard in her cleaning job and barely supported herself and her deadbeat drunken husband. All the while this fashion plate buzzed merrily around, full of energy, immensely enjoying her volunteer position. Nurse's aide. HA! Always in her crisp uniform, more of a good will ambassador cheering up the patients than a true worker.

Madame Tussaud managed a phony smile whenever they spoke and usually made it a point to pick up a scrap of information that could prove useful. A typical conversation began in this manner. "Good morning Mme. Pontmercy, how are you and your family?" Over a period of a few weeks she was able to extract answers to questions such as: What does your husband do for a living? Where do you live? And how many children do you have?

After concluding the Pontmercy's were very well off financially, Madame Tussaud engaged the devious part of her mind. Her less than ambitious husband, Claude, had a sinister friend whom she had met on a few occasions. Rousseau drank considerably less than her husband and had a knack for obtaining expensive items without maintaining a regular job. Once Madame Tussaud was approached by Rousseau asking, "I know yer behind in yer rent. How many francs do you need?" She soon found out that the majority of his income was not gained by honest methods.

So, along with her husband and Rousseau, Mme. Tussaud concocted the plan to kidnap Cosette. Actually the plan was fairly simple. Cosette came to the hospital for her nurse's aide volunteer work quite faithfully every Wednesday. With an in house nanny, it was no problem for her to spend time outside the home, even with two children. It was known for some time that Cosette traveled by fiacre both to and from the hospital. A walk that would take nearly an hour was pared down to 15 minutes for a price considered negligible by the Pontmercy's.

Madame asked Cosette one day, "Do you have an agreement of some kind with the cab company? I notice it's always there for you right on time." "Oh yes," was the reply. "They're very punctual and my husband is acquainted with the owner." "Isn't that nice," Madame continued with a barely detectable arrogance, "Is it always the same driver too?" "Quite often, but not always," the unknowingly cooperative Cosette said, "They have a few drivers that alternate."

Another piece of the plot fit nicely into place. The driver of the fiacre would be disposed of with a blow to the head and then bound and gagged and his place taken by Rousseau with Claude inside the cab as the only other passenger. It would be carried out on a cool rainy day with both men bundled up to reduce the probability of identification. By the time Cosette realized she was not headed in the direction of her house it would be too late. She could easily be overpowered and taken to the place of her imprisonment and the ransom note prepared. One hundred thousand francs! Mme. Tussaud couldn't wait. The trio could live very comfortably for a long time on that amount. She planned to stay on for at least a month at the hospital, to avoid any possible suspicion, and then find some reason to quit the job she hated.

A few weeks later Marius and Cosette were having breakfast and talking about the weather. It was a Wednesday in mid October.

"It seems to be a beautiful morning 'Dear," Cosette exclaimed. "True, my love," replied Marius. "It's a little damp though, some of my joints tell me some rain could be on the way. Do dress Jean warmly for his classes."

"Of course, and I'll be sure to take my rain coat to the hospital, even if it's dry when I leave the house."

"Fine, and I'll be thinking of you often as I pour through the books in preparation for my next case."

At 8:45 the cab arrived as usual for Cosette. Clouds were thickening and upon reaching the hospital she was sure it was a little darker outdoors than it had been an hour earlier. Cosette greeted her co-workers and fell into the routine of the day, just as she always did.

Mme. Tussaud acted more friendly and talkative than her usual self. She used visions of wealth and power to overcome some mild nervousness as the time of reckoning drew near. All of Paris will be buzzing by this time tomorrow she mused silently to herself.

Lunch time came and went as the unsuspecting Cosette's work day was winding down. The weather had indeed turned nastier as rain arrived and a raw wind increased in strength.

At approximately twenty till 3:00 a glance outside revealed the fiacre had arrived and was waiting. Cosette donned her rain gear and departed the hospital.

"Afternoon," muttered the driver as Cosette boarded the cab. "Why, hello, I don't believe we've met" was the reply. "No, I'm new on this job."

Once inside the cab, Cosette saw that there was one other passenger on board. Every so often one or two people were already on board so Cosette was not alarmed and said, "Hello Monsieur." The passenger, who appeared somewhat disheveled and quite wet, grunted an unintelligible reply. Cosette turned and looked out the window at the rain.

A few minutes later a hand appeared and closed Cosette's curtain over her window. Before she had time to demand an explanation, that same hand, belonging to the passenger, clamped roughly over her mouth as the coach came to an abrupt halt. By the time she tried to react or begin to struggle, Rousseau the driver lunged into the cab began tying her hands and ankles. Rousseau, having heard much of the victims beauty during the kidnap planning, acquainted himself rather nonchalantly with the calf area of the victims legs without her realizing it. Supposing himself to be quite a ladies man, he vowed to himself to extend his familiarity with the victims anatomy if the opportunity presented itself during captivity. This would be attempted only after the ransom money was extorted and he felt there was nothing to lose.

Cosette was now trembling, both with fear of her current situation and also the cold and dampness of the afternoon. Blindfolded by this time she could not tell where she was going although she realized that the ride was much longer than the usual trip home.

The passenger, Claude Tussaud, leaned out the door and shouted to Rousseau, "How much further?" "It will not be long now," he replied. Their destination was a deserted building near the river where they would remain until they were joined by the third member of their group. Then, after the cover of darkness had arrived, they would move their high priced cargo to the place of her captivity until the 100,000 franc ransome was paid. Upon their arrival Rousseau declared, "I'm going to dispose of the cab now. I'll return in about a half hour. "

"Be careful" Claude said as he left.

As Claude removed Cosette's gag and blindfold, he issued a stern warning, "One scream and this goes back on, understand?" Cosette understood perfectly and could only stammer, "What do you fiends want with me?" "Don't you know, you're going to make us rich. You won't be hurt, provided your wealthy husband pays us 100,000 francs! Are you worth that much to the Baron Pontmercy? Oh, I'm sure you are, and probably much more."

"He'll go to the authorities and I'll be rescued," Cosette said. You monsters will go to prison for a very long time."

"We'll see about that, Princess, just don't get your hopes up."

Claude began building a fire in the old building's fireplace as it was cold and damp. By the time he had a warm blaze started, the door opened and two figures entered. Cosette looked past Rousseau to the next person and felt a chill through her whole body as she immediately recognized Mme. Tussaud.

"Don't look so surprised rich lady," stated Mme. Tussaud, "you've got more money than you can use and we're going to have some of it."

"Please don't do this," Cosette said half sobbing. "My family will be devastated and you won't get away with it anyway. Marius will see to that."

"The rich baron will see to nothing except producing 100,000 francs in a big hurry." Rousseau had begun to add his comments.

"My sources say he's worth half a million at least. Once he gets our note it won't take him very long — not if he wants you back that is."

Later, after a meager meal, the time had arrived to take the captive to the designated place to be held for the duration of the scheme. The ransome note would be delivered tied to a rock and thrown through a ground floor window at the Pontmercy House.

Mme. Tussaud and Rousseau took Cosette toward the river while Claude arranged for the ransome note to be delivered.

When Marius left for work earlier that morning, he was expecting a routine fall day. Within the next few hours he would be ushered into circumstances beyond his control. As Nicolette was away visiting relatives, it was Marie who met Marius with a concerned look on her face. "I was hoping Cosette was with you, M. Marius, she hasn't returned yet from the hospital." "Why no, Marie, perhaps she was detained." "But that's not like her. Should I hold dinner, it will be ready soon?" "Delay dinner a while, and by the way, how are the children today?" "They're fine. Jean did well with his reading class and Ponine re-arranged her doll house about a dozen times."

Marius peered out the window at the rain and said, "If Cosette's not home within 30 minutes, I'll get transportation to the hospital and find out the reason for her delay."

"Good idea, M. Marius, the children and I will feel much better when she arrives."

Shortly after arriving at the hospital his optimism about the situation quickly evaporated. "Mme. Renaud, what time did Cosette leave today?" Marius inquired. "The same time she always does. Why do you ask, M. Pontmercy?"

"Cosette has not returned home as of yet and I'm becoming more concerned with each passing minute."

Just then a tall, official-looking figure entered the lobby. "Inspector Marchand — who's in charge here?" After the initial formalities, Marchand declared his reason for being there. "A fiacre was stolen and the driver assaulted, can anyone here shed some light on this? He was last seen near the hospital."

With that revelation Marius's heart sank. He sensed a connection with Cosette's apparent disappearance.

"Inspector, my wife usually rides that fiacre and she hasn't been seen for almost three hours now," Marius interjected.

"We'll leave immediately for your residence, Monsieur?" "Pontmercy" Marius answered as they hurried toward the door.

On the way Marius answered Marchand's queries relative to Cosette's work at the hospital and her hours. Upon nearing the front door, Marie came bounding out of the house clutching a piece of paper in her hand.

HIS WORST FEARS REALIZED

"M. Marius - they have her, they have her!" cried Marie. "Calm down Marie, who has her?" Marius asked, almost in unison with the inspector. "Here! See for yourself. Read this note. Oh Lord, this is horrible."

Marius and inspector Marchand read the note together. The note stated:

> Baron Pontmercy - We have your wife! She will
> not be harmed if you cooperate. Get 100,000 francs
> from the bank—Wait for instructions tomorrow.

Marchand studied the note and said to Marius, "Don't worry Monsieur, your house will be watched for the next rock thrower. Standby officers will be active for extra patrols and questioning of suspects. We have ways to gather information from the underworld of this city."

Marius was not very reassured although he nodded sadly to the inspector, "What can I do to help, Inspector?"

"Go to the bank tomorrow morning early and withdraw the required amount - then stay home in case they attempt to contact you. I suppose you have the funds?"

"Yes, of course, somehow these kidnappers must have known" said Marius.

"Hard to say," replied the inspector "They could be bluffing on the amount demanded. Try to get some rest now and I'll contact you in the morning."

Cosette and the criminal pair were indeed approaching the river but she saw no boat of any type and was filled with apprehension. She was bound at the hands and gagged, but not blindfolded.

"Move along my pretty," said Madame Tussaud "Down to the left." However, there was nothing in that direction, Cosette thought to herself, nothing but a sewer grating. That grating seemed exactly what they were headed for and, upon reaching it, appeared more massive and taller than she expected.

"Get it open quickly," Mme. Tussaud said to Rousseau. "We must not be seen, you know."

Once inside Cosette's heart sank even further. What a foul and disgusting place to be. And, dear God, how long must I be here. Oh no, they'll never find me in a place like this.

Once inside they moved toward the right where the ground sloped upward and was dry. About 30 feet in that direction was a wall and a fairly flat area approximately eight feet long and four feet wide. With the small lantern Rousseau carried, Cosette saw a narrow cot, a blanket, and a jug of water. So this was it. The place of her captivity. She thought back to a happy morning and an enjoyable time at the hospital. What a difference a few hours made. How much Marius and the children were missed already and this was probably only the beginning. How long would it take Marius to obtain the ransome money? Would the transaction with the kidnappers go smoothly and her release according to plan? Could there be a double-cross where she would be abandoned and left to die? These were the thoughts foremost in Cosette's mind.

"How do you like your new apartment?" snarled Mme. Tussaud. Without waiting for a reply she continued, "Make yourself right at home. I'm going down to the main sewer line from the city and check the levels. We've had a rainy day and we don't want you floating away on us, now do we."

Cosette cringed at the thought, but answered with some courage "Give this up. Can't you see it won't work and you'll spend the rest of your lives in prison?"

"Our plan will work," Rousseau chimed in at that point. "The authorities haven't caught up with me for five years and I don't think that will change now. Sit down on the cot now, I have to tie your feet soon."

Mme. Tussaud was out of sight on her patrol by this time and Rousseau drew nearer to the prisoner. Hovering over her, he was rethinking his carnal desires that he entertained earlier in the day. This lovely and quite helpless woman was definitely more desirable right now then she would be after spending a day or two in this fetid cavern. After deliberating the situation for a few brief moments he decided to take full advantage of his powerful position. Just as his hands were beginning to untie; unhook, unclutter and undress, instead of tying two feet together, Mme. Tussaud returned to the scene. "What do you think you're doing, fool?" she shrieked. "I'll have no damaged goods here. Move aside — I'll finish tying her up. Don't forget whose idea this was and whose giving the orders here. Don't forget it for a minute."

Rousseau backed off grudgingly. He picked up the lantern as they were ready to leave and said nothing. Mme. Tussaud gave Cosette water from the jug and said as they left, "We'll be back in the morning with some breakfast. See that you don't go anywhere!" After a morbid chuckle that echoed through the caverns she bellowed, "And sleep well."

Marius didn't sleep well, to be sure. In fact he didn't sleep at all as he tossed and turned all night thinking about the perilous situation in which Cosette obviously found herself. He listened to the rain which just refused to leave the area. At dawn he rose and forced down some bread and coffee. After dressing he responded hurriedly to a knock on the door surmising it to be Inspector Marchand. Instead he has confronted with a gamin he had seen before roaming the streets of the city.

"Monsieur Pontmercy, I have a letter for you. Quite important I'd say. I can eat for a month on the proceeds of this errand. Good day to you." "Not so fast young man," Marius responded, "Who gave you this letter?" "Don't really know, the gamin replied. "It was still quite dark and his hat pulled down low. Average height — maybe 30 or 35 years old. Didn't care much when I saw the color of his money. Leavin' now — got a friend who's hungry and so am I."

Marius ripped open the envelope and read the following:

> Bring 100,000 francs to the old mill bridge
> north west of town in a burlap sack. Come alone,
> no police, the area will be watched. Alone — or
> the deal's off and you'll never see your wife again.
> Come at noon and be on time."

No sooner had Marius read the note for the third time when Marchand arrived on the scene along with an officer. Marius showed them the note and said, "I must follow these instructions. Please don't interfere Inspector. Cosette's safety depends on it." "It could be a trap, Monsieur. The police should handle this and you may have your wife back and keep your money as well." "Not a chance. I can't risk my wife's life on that plan of action. After she's returned safely, you can pursue them and prosecute to the fullest extent of the law." "Very well, we'll stay out of the general area, but my men and I will never be very far away." "Fine," Marius concluded, "It's settled then. I'll pick up the currency around eleven and be at the bridge by noon."

The Tussands arrived at the sewer around 8:00, leaving the amorous Rousseau behind to see to other details of the plot. They found Cosette shivering uncontrollably under her less than adequate covering. "Rise and shine deary," said Mme. Tussaud gruffly. "Here's your breakfast, get it while it's hot." "What's this?" said Claude, "Been workin' on your ropes, huh. Almost got loose did you. Couldn't really go far but we can't have you yelling through the grating can we. You shouldn't be here much longer if everything goes well for us. For now though, we'll make these ropes much tighter. After breakfast of course."

Cosette's meal consisted of lukewarm coffee, some bread and cheese. She dared not complain though, fearful for her life and also a growing dread of Rousseau. She mustered up some courage and asked, "When will I be released? Did you get your money yet? You'll never get away with this you know."

"Hush up and eat quickly and when you're done put these clothes on," said Mme. Tussaud as she produced a sack containing some tasteless women's clothing which appeared to be near her size. Claude looked at the clothes with almost as much amazement as Cosette, but he said nothing then. It was obviously a new twist in the plot which he hadn't been consulted for input. Cosette's outfit was put in the sack which they had brought.

After Cosette was retied more securely the pair prepared to leave and Madame said to the prisoner, "We'll be back for you in about three hours. Don't get too ambitious and spoil your chance for freedom." They both grumbled about the rain as they left the river area.

Cosette wasn't thinking about freedom right then, only about keeping the circulation in her arms and legs up to par with the new and punishing bonds which held her. She could only pray that her release would come soon after they came for her in three hours.

THE FOUR HORSEMEN

Four of the most evil men in Paris were an underworld group known as the Four Horsemen. No one knew for sure if they earned their name from the Four Horsemen of the apocalypse or the fact that they sometimes used horses when escaping from the outskirts of the city to their country hideouts. They were well acquainted with death and pestilence to be sure and were blamed for many crimes they did not commit. However, they committed enough mayhem on their own to deserve whatever aliases they acquired. All four were wanted by the law, all had been in prison, two served their time and two had escaped. All were rugged and at or above average height and weight.

How does this unsavory group fit into the story? We will now find out. Rosseau, along with his weakness for the fairer sex, also had a penchant for gambling. One lost weekend some months back, he lost heavily to one of the horsemen and owed 300 francs. They hounded him constantly and apparently compounded the interest quite regularly, the amount had grown to 600 francs and Rousseau knew he had to do something soon in order to go on living, which he had a strong liking for.

He had recently thought long and hard about a robbery he could consummate. Before any plans were solidified he fell into the kidnap plot with the Tussauds. His share of the ransome money would pay off the horsemen and get them out of his life forever. He had even thought of leaving the city and buying a small farm further south.

Although Rousseau was not aware, for the last week or two at least one of the horsemen kept fairly close tabs on him. They usually knew his general whereabouts and noticed his peculiar behavior in recent days. The kidnapping was a big news item in the city and the group had enough criminal intuition to suspect Rousseau was involved. They would be watching events closely.

Marius had no trouble at all withdrawing the necessary funds from the bank. Monsieur Cartier said to him, "Our prayers are with you young man. This ordeal will soon be behind you."

"Thank you, ever so much. It was very kind of you to rush this request through. I must go quickly — good day."

Inspector Marchand met Marius outside the bank and asked, "Did you make your withdrawal satisfactorily?" "Yes. I believe I'm now ready to make the transfer and get my wife back from those who have her. You and your men will keep far enough away to cause no suspicion, I presume."

"There are twelve deputies in the area working in Paris. They will be discreet until after your wife is safely back, and then make their presence known on all roads in the vicinity. I think we stand a good chance of apprehending the villain or villains whatever the case may be. It would be a real coup to have your wife and money too, eh Monsieur." "My wife first and foremost and the money is, of course, secondary, my good man," Marius said as he started his walk toward the bridge.

The plan Mme. Tussaud recently modified included the following twist. She feared the possibility of receiving a bag filled with papers or other worthless material instead of the ransome money. The captive would then be reunited with her family and they would have no pay off. With the scenario she devised a substitute person would be released and if the money was given as instructed the hostage could be released later, or perhaps held for even more bounty.

She concluded the update to her husband with following remarks, "Rousseau by this time has enlisted the services of a former girlfriend about the same height as the 'princess' and will have her standing by to change into the dress in this sack. As her head will be hooded, which M. the baron will assume is mainly a blindfold, we will appropriate the bag of money and melt into the wooded area nearby. The same young gamin who delivered the ransome note will gather the sack and deliver it to us with haste. By the time the rich man discovers what happened, we will be gone. If we are tricked and get no money, we will be no worse off."

"Brilliant, my dear, how your mind works. I knew I married you for something."

"By the way, we are going over to Rousseau's flat to divide the money and hide out until nightfall," added the brains of the group.

It was shortly before noon when Marius neared the old mill bridge. He saw nobody, and was grateful that included no policemen. The rain had abated temporarily with only a fine mist in the air, although there was no sign yet for a general clearing in the weather.

After a short while he noticed movement by the trees north of the bridge. He left his vantage point on the bridge itself and walked in that direction. Now he saw more clearly two figures emerging and coming in his direction. It was Cosette and a young boy. Was that the same boy escorting his wife who had delivered the ransome note, he wondered. And why was her head covered? Was she kept like that for two days? He hoped not. At least he recognized her dress as they got within 40 yards.

Suddenly the gamin left his escort and dashed toward Marius. "There she is Monsieur, I'll take that bag and be gone." Marius, somewhat surprised, left go of the bag and trotted toward Cosette. She was standing in the same spot with her hands tied behind her back and unable to see.

Marius reached her and first removed the hood. "Darling, I missed you _ _ _" Marius stopped in mid-sentence. Taken completely aback and shocked, "You're not my wife. Who are you and what's going on here?"

"Sorry Monsieur, I just did a favor for an old friend. He gave me twenty francs too. Quite a guy."

By this time Marius was furious. He also smelled cheap spirits on this woman's breath. "Get out of here barfly," Marius snapped. "You'll be hearing from the authorities about this. You're now involved in a kidnapping, that's some friend you have."

THE LAIR OF DEATH

The trio of kidnappers, anticipating the worst and expecting the police at every crossroad, walked briskly through the wooded area on a little used nature path and emerged over a mile away. A quick glance in the bag told them it surely contained money, although they didn't know how much and weren't about to count it until later.

It was decided they would split up as they reached the public streets, with Madame Tussaud carrying the bag. She hoped the bank notes were not too large because the sack appeared to be lighter than she imagined. The larger bills would attract more attention when they were spent by people from their side of town.

In a little less than an hour all three reached Rousseau's flat. He fired up the stove as it was cool and damp. The rain, heavy at times, was now well into it's second day. The curtains in the small, sparsely furnished apartment had not been opened earlier and they remain closed now. The door was bolted by Rousseau, who turned and said, "Dump the bag on that table, no need to wait for dark on a day like this. I'll light the lamp and keep it turned down low." "Why not?" returned Madame Tussaud. "We couldn't wait two or three more hours anyway to check this out. But don't forget, Claude and I will need to stay here until after dark, before we return home." "Suit yourselves, but I want my share now! I have things to do."

In reality the contents of the bag were all the same, 200 bills of 500 francs each. They must have counted it three times just to be sure. The booty was just in the process of being stacked in three piles when Rousseau thought he heard something outside. He said, as the three became instantly silent, "Must have been the wind or the rain." The other two agreed.

They knew they were wrong an instant later when the door burst open with a tremendous thud. The well worn latch and bolt were no match for the powerful thrust of two of The Four Horsemen simultaneously. Soon the awful quartet were all in the room with the door wedged back in a closed position.

"Aha, what have we here Rousseau? And who are your two friends?" asked the leader.

The startled kidnappers were frozen for an instant after the intrusion. Now Rousseau rose and said, "Back off, I have your money. I was going to look you up this very day."

"Looks like you have more than you need on that table," said a second horseman.

"Not so," Rousseau replied. "We've earned this at great risk." He was getting nervous, knowing these men were always heavily armed.

When two of the horsemen started reaching for weapons all hell broke loose. The two male members of the kidnappers were also armed, while Mme. Tussaud darted toward the bedroom, hoping to escape via a window and temporarily withdrawing any claim she had for the money. Shots rang out and Claude fell first. Rousseau knocked the money table over and dove behind it. He got off two shots before being fatally hit himself. Claude failed to get a shot off before taking two mortal body hits. Mme. Tussaud made it to the bedroom window and no further. A lethal shot to the back of the head ended her escape attempt and she slumped backward to the floor.

By the time the smoke cleared The Four Horsemen had become The Three Horsemen. Rousseau had made his shots count as one of the remaining horsemen would probably never have full use of his left arm again, having taken a gruesome shoulder wound. However, all three kidnappers were dead and lying in pools of their own blood.

Thus, the situation was as follows, the ransome money had again changed hands, while the hostage had not. The three people who knew where the victim of the kidnapping was, were now dead. What will become of poor Cosette now.

The optimism experienced by Cosette earlier in the day was diminishing quickly. Although she didn't know the exact time, it was obvious the kidnappers were far behind schedule. The indirect daylight that was observed indicated the afternoon light was fading fast. She was sore from her bindings, very cold and hungry and was now coughing and feeling the effects of her insidious confinement.

Despite all that was just related, Cosette now entertained a new and potentially deadly problem. The sewer itself had not been a threat, other than the odor and dampness. However, with the two days of rainfall added to the normal sewer volume, the situation was changing rapidly. She heard ominous gurgling sounds and could vaguely see the water line inching closer to the small cul-de-sac where she was virtually immobilized.

Shortly after the ill-fated transfer of funds for an imposter, Marius was joined by Inspector Marchand. "We have the woman, Monsieur, but no word on the kidnappers as of now. I'm convinced she knows nothing — just a pawn in this whole affair. My men are combing the area, keep up the faith, we'll soon find out how successful they were."

"This is all very frustrating, Marchand. Perhaps I should have allowed you to operate closer to the scene. This is not fair to my wife or myself. We kept our part of the bargain and now I'm not sure of anything."

"Go home Monsieur. Go home, rest and wait, and who knows, more notes may be delivered. Your wife may arrive there, after they've counted the money and are satisfied, they may release her. I will advise you as soon as I learn anything helpful."

"Very well Inspector. I'll go home and collect my thoughts and make my plans. By tomorrow morning I'll be searching as well. Whatever you say or do will not stop me, so please don't try. I'm sure Cosette is in serious danger by now."

In the dark, Cosette could not see the level of the water rising, she could sense it though. The lightly swirling tide, which was mostly rain water runoff, would prove just as lethal as the more disgusting refuse, should the level continue to rise.

Her anxiety increasing, the hostage thought, or rather prayed, "Dear Lord, don't let me die this way — drowning in this place. I'm sure Marius would survive, but the children, it would be devastating for them."

Cosette had not eaten or drank since that morning and was craving food and/or water. After a great deal of effort she swung her legs over the edge of the cot and grasped the water jug. Slowly and carefully, with her hands still tied, she lifted the jug until she was able to bite on the cork stopper and remove it. Water trickled down her face and some into her mouth. She had consumed about four or five ounces when the jug slipped from her grip and fell to the floor. It didn't shatter but rolled away out of sight and most of it's contents wasted.

She tried to find it but after a few steps recoiled in horror. The water level reached her feet and she hurried back to the cot and slightly higher ground. The end seemed near but Cosette vowed to rack her brain for any slim hope of survival that might be available to her.

Early the next morning Marius, along with Marcel, made their way to the police station to see Inspector Marchand. They were both pleased to observe that the infernal rain had subsided after three days.

"Good morning Monsieur," the Inspector said mechanically. Marius could tell in an instant there was no helpful information gained during the night. Regardless he asked, "What are your plans for today, Inspector?" "We have some leads — nothing definite. My twelve men will be joined by a squad of twenty reserves of the military. The latter will be investigating known hideouts and scouring nearby countryside."

"Marcel and I will be searching today as well. I can't just sit at home waiting and depending on others. It's nerve wracking and tortuous."

"By the way M. Pontmercy, there was major underworld violence yesterday afternoon. A triple murder! One of the victims had a police record, the other two were a married couple with no prior criminal records. We're looking into this as quickly as possible. The man was a part-time handyman, but the woman was an employee at Paris General Hospital. Perhaps an acquaintance of your wife, we will find out soon.

"Keep me posted as best you can, Inspector. We expect to be out until early afternoon and then stop home briefly. After that, who knows, probably until well past dark."

"Good hunting Monsieur," said Marchand. "Maybe our luck will change now that the rain has stopped."

AS HOPE BEGINS TO FADE

Cosette huddled on her cot throughout the night as the water level kept creeping closer. Her cough was more frequent and raspier. Shortly before dawn the life-threatening tide reached the very legs of her cot, but there it stopped. Just when all seemed hopeless a divine providence smiled down on the prisoner. Although she had no way of knowing, the rain had ceased about two hours earlier. The level held constant for several hours and then began to slowly recede.

Gradually sensing what was happening temporarily eased Cosette's anxiety. Her life was spared for the moment only, the thirst and hunger were still present although now her hunger was blurred by chills and cramps in her limbs. She knew a fever was present as the chills caused her to tremble violently at times. In a time of mild delirium she muttered out loud, "Father (Jean Valjean) where are you now? Why can't Marius and the police find me? I must get out of this place and find the children. Jean and Ponine — Have you finished supper yet."

As she had not slept all night, she dropped off briefly to a restless sleep, interrupted from time to time with fits of coughing.

Marcel, growing weary from hours of walking tapped Marius on the shoulder, "Well" was the only response. "It's mid-afternoon, M. Marius, we must go home and rest a bit and have some lunch. It could be the Inspector has left a message for us or he may be there in person."

"Of course you're right Marcel, I've been tough on you these past few days. We must keep up our strength until this ordeal is over."

They had covered several miles from the hospital and around the old mill bridge and the nearby wooded area. At least a dozen times they talked with people on the street, hoping to gain a scrap of information or a clue of some type. Twice they noticed some of the reserves Marchand had enlisted in the search.

When they reached home they learned from Marie the Inspector had not been there nor had she received a message of any kind. She did have a lunch prepared for them and Marcel stretched out for a time as he was in desperate need for "forty winks." Marius napped as well for he wanted to be fresh enough to search well into the evening.

A long fit of coughing roused Cosette as she felt herself growing weaker in what seemed to be a losing battle. Where were her captors she thought. What went wrong with their plot? Is it possible they got the ransome money and left the area entirely? Were they captured by the authorities and refused to talk?

These thoughts were constantly on her mind as she noticed that daylight was slowly beginning to fade. Just then she thought she heard something. A sound unlike the flowing and swirling water that threatened her earlier. A kind of scratching sound continued to become more and more evident. Was her mind playing tricks on her now she wondered. Could her temperature be that high from the fever?

Moments later, Cosette knew that was not the case at all. To her complete chagrin, peering directly ahead from her cot, not more than four feet away was the largest rat she had ever seen. Her body, long since drained of adrenaline, became limp as all strength was depleted. The next horror was a nibbling sensation at her feet. There must be another one at the end of her cot she surmised. The last thing she remembered was trying to kick and move her feet, before lapsing into unconsciousness.

Marius did not nap long. He dreamed of life without Cosette and it seemed devastating. The children growing up without a mother. A life without love for himself. His dreams drifted to the barricade, to his old friends from the A,BC. They had all died, his dream was morbid. He should have died himself that day, were it not for Cosette's guardian. In the worst day of his life he was carried from a barricade and through a sewer to medical help and survival.

He woke up with a start. "Marcel, we must leave, and bring the bolt cutters along with the two lanterns. We'll probably be out late and I want to swing by the sewer outlet before we return home."

Marcel thought the last request strange, but obeyed. "I can be ready in five minutes. Marie has some bread and wine packed also."

More fruitless searching, more blind alleys confronted them. Marius was completely discouraged by dusk but he remained determined to check around the sewer before quitting for the day. Hadn't every other place in the city been checked already? The bolt cutters sliced through the chain holding the grating in place. Then Marius, with Marcel behind, entered the very sewer from whence he came, in his own wretched condition, some years ago.

Once inside, Marius moved toward the left while Marcel headed the opposite direction. He had barely gone a dozen steps when he heard Marcel cry out. "Over here! Come quickly!"

It was fortunate for Cosette that only about twenty minutes elapsed from the time she fainted and the arrival of Marius and

Marcel. Her inner strength and will to live kept her moving in an attempt to hold the rats at bay. The rodents apparently were used to having their victims quite dead and motionless. Even so, when Marcel burst onto the scene the giant rat was only a few inches from that once dazzling countenance. Several others were already up on the cot probing for an opening. One nasty medium size rat had fastened his teeth on Cosette's foot. All but the latter scattered into the darkness rather quickly with light and sounds now present.

Marcel had just started flailing at the stubborn one with the bolt cutters when Marius entered the cul-de-sac. Marius was aghast on his arrival and asked Marcel, "Are we too late?" "I don't know M. Marius, bring the other lantern closer."

"She looks terrible Marcel, let's untie her first and then get her out of here quickly. Take one lantern and go on ahead. Find the first fiacre and compel the driver to come here. We have an urgent medical emergency."

As Marcel moved hurriedly on, Marius spoke to his still unconscious wife. "Hold on my precious love, you're going to live, you can't leave me now. Soon you'll be in the hospital where you can rest and have food and water."

Marius thought he saw Cosette's eyes flutter open for an instant and then close as he gathered her up in his arms. He made his way carefully with the lantern handle hooked around his arm, not wanting to trip in that area. Soon they were out in the cool evening air and Marius noticed her labored and wheezy breathing. He looked around for Marcel and the cab they needed quickly. Within ten minutes one arrived and all three were on their way to the hospital where this predicament began not many days ago.

Cosette was still not out of danger. It was determined at the hospital she had pneumonia and a high fever. There was also an infection present, due to rodent bites and exposure and dehydration. Marius, on leave from his job, spent many hours by her side. The doctors knew that the fever must break soon for her to recover. One cannot survive very long in that condition of semi-consciousness and delirium.

After her second day of hospitalization, Cosette appeared to take a turn for the worse. Word was sent for Marius to come earlier than the regular visiting hours. By the time he arrived, Cosette was lucid for the first time in several days. Her fever had peaked to its highest point just before breaking. The hospital stay required two more weeks for the infection to leave and her strength to return to a near-normal threshold.

By the time she was feeling better, Cosette asked Marius countless questions relative to the whole incident. Her memory was blurry after the first day of captivity and she wanted to know about everything that occurred during the investigation and search by the police and Marius. She was, of course, shocked to learn of the death of the Tussauds and the involvement of The Four Horsemen.

Inspector Marchand paid them a visit one evening and related everything the police were able to piece together. The discovery of the burlap bag and two of the bank notes at Rousseau's place confirmed their suspicions. The Horseman who was wounded was arrested when he sought medical attention, while the remaining two were still at large.

As he prepared to leave Marchand said, "Sorry we have not recovered the majority of the ransome money as of yet, but we are working on it."

Marius chuckled softly and replied, "That's quite alright Inspector, I have my beloved wife back. The money can be replaced, but I have someone here far more precious than any amount of money. Good evening to you, Monsieur."

Eventually Cosette recovered fully and life found its way back to normalcy for the Pontmercy's. The children were growing, and they flourished. Marius encountered four or five interesting and challenging cases, for every dull and boring one. The family lived well but never to extravagance. And they thanked their creator for their many blessings. The city of Paris struggled inexorably on, through its half-century of turmoil. There were peaks and valleys to be sure, but toward the end of the first half of the nineteenth century, misery and trouble began once again to rear its ugly head.

And if any mischief follow, then thou shalt give life for life, eye for eye, tooth for tooth, hand for hand, foot for foot.

Ex. 21:23, 24

Chapter IV

1848

. . . .

CAMP LAFAYETTE

Before delving into the mayhem which transpired during the first half of 1848, climaxing in the month of June, it seems logical to bring the reader up to date relative to the lives of the Pontmercy children. Keep in mind Jean and Eponine were approximately 12 1/2 and 10 1/2 respectively at the time new hostilities were surely and steadily moving toward their boiling point.

Actually, two summers prior to this, the children's two week stay at Camp Lafayette provided the only deviation from the mundane in the lives of the children, or the Pontmercy family in general since the kidnapping incident very early in the decade.

It began when Marius announced his brainstorm, "Cosette darling, during our business luncheon today several friends and acquaintances were discussing plans to send their children to summer camp. Camp Lafayette, just three miles south of the city. Many of the professional families have sent their boys and girls there before and they loved it. The camp runs for two weeks and accepts children ages six to fourteen."

"Oh Marius, I don't know. Two weeks seems like such a long time. I'd miss them terribly. When does it begin, anyway?"

"In just two weeks. The last week in July and the first week of August. It's a fine way to revitalize the lazy summer days for them."

"Suppose they're not interested," Cosette continued with somewhat less resolve.

"Well, let's check with them and see. They must be registered soon if they plan to attend."

Of course they were more than interested, they were delighted, especially when they learned the camp had a distinctive farm-like setting. It would be hard to find two city kids who were not interested in spending some time in the country around a large number of farm animals. The Pontmercy Home was destined for a quiet and peaceful two weeks. Or was it?

For the first week everything went well. The milking of the cows; the feeding of the pigs, the pony rides and, of course, the friendly dogs and cats kept their interest intact. However, as the second week got underway some of that interest was waning.

Eponine whispered to her new-found friend, Arlette, also a newcomer at the camp, "I want to go home." "So do I," was the reply, followed by "And I know the way." "Good, because I don't." "I live nearby. We'll go to my place first," added Arlette. "Right after lunch," concluded Eponine as the little conference ended.

After the noon meal the girls, bringing nothing with them, walked to the end of the corn field and, seeing no one watching, kept right on walking toward the road that led to the camp. It was a warm sunny day with some puffy white clouds and not a hint of rain. The camp road was barely a half-mile long and then came an intersection with a larger thoroughfare which ran north and south.

"Arlette, are you sure you know the way?" Eponine asked. "I think we turn left here, Ponine." "I hope so. You know, we should hide when people pass by. They might take us right back to the farm." And so the girls remained undetected as they made their way further south, instead of travelling north in the direction of Paris and home. Arlette had guessed wrong and they were going toward the town of Evry.

The afternoon passed quickly and it seemed every time a wagon or a coach loomed in their vicinity and they ran off the road, a patch of raspberries or blackberries was just a stone's throw away. It must be said that their small hands and faces began to take on the color of those delicious berries as well.

Before long Arlette admitted, "We should have gotten to my place by now. Think we should go back?" "Let's keep going — It won't be dark for a long time. I'm not scared, are you?" A barely audible 'no' followed and they were on their way again.

It was almost two hours before the girls were missed at camp. Much of the afternoon was designated as 'free time' for the children and there were 32 enrolled there of various ages. The camp staff searched the grounds with the help of several fourteen year old boys, but without success. The next step was the half hour ride to the city and the work places of the fathers of the missing children. Marius returned with the camp owner and Arlette's father was out of the area on business. They immediately made plans for a more extensive search.

As dusk began to settle on the countryside the girls began to feel chilly in addition to a growing concern as to their whereabouts. Their thirst had been quenched recently by a small stream and they consumed so many berries hunger was not a serious problem. Eponine spotted a small elevation in the terrain and said, while running toward it, "Let's climb up this hill and look for houses." As Arlette started up the hill on the far side, something else caught her attention. "There's a cave here, Ponine." "Oh, I'm coming over, wait there." "I think we better stay here. It's getting much darker." Eponine picked up a large stick and said, "We might need this to fight wild animals." "I hope not. We'll go back soon as it's light tomorrow," Arlette said as the pair huddled closer together to stay warm.

By this time the search party was nearly through for the evening as well. They had no luck in searching within a half mile radius of the farm. In the morning there would be almost 100 volunteers combing the area and there was a great deal of confidence of finding the girls in good condition. The weather was fine and there was no sign of foul play and after further investigation, the camp was found to have an incident like this every year or so.

Thankfully, such was the case. Shortly before 8:00 a.m. the girls were seen trying to retrace their steps along the road and this time they didn't try to hide. In fact they were very happy to see a local farmer and his wife who were part of the volunteer search party.

Marius was so happy to see his angel safe and well that he put away his earlier thoughts of punishment for their little escapade which caused so many concerns. Eponine did return home immediately but Jean insisted on finishing his second week at the camp which he was thoroughly enjoying.

1848 (AND A BIT OF HISTORY)

As the city of Paris seethed in turmoil, in early June, 1848, young Jean Pontmercy posed a question. "Father, will you be going to the barricades this time?" "Now Jean, what makes you think there will be barricades?" "I know all about barricades and I've heard you and mother talking about street fighting down town." "That's a strong possibility, son, but these problems could all be settled peacefully."

"What do you really think will happen father? You were there last time and I've heard your stories." "Well Jean, that was 16 years ago, but things haven't changed all that much. The mood of the city is very ugly. I'm afraid fighting could break out at any time. Most of the men I work with feel the same way as I do." "Father, last time you fought against the police and the military. Why was that?" "Like I said, son, that was a long time ago and I was a single man at the time. I had many friends who were also students and they had dreams of a new and better France. A whole new world for that matter. Our weapons weren't the best though and we had no training of any sort. There was precious little ammunition or food supplies at the barricades as well. But to answer your first question, no, I won't be going to the barricades this time. When you're a little older, son, you'll understand what it means to have a family and responsibilities. I believe God really spared my life years ago to raise a family and become a lawyer and help the people of Paris. Some of the poorer people in the city don't know the law too well and can't always pay me right away, but that's the type of citizen that needs my services the most. So, I hope you can understand when I tell you that I'm not in a position to take part in the fighting, if indeed it comes to that. I'll be taking care of your mother and your sister and the others that count on me."

"I think I understand father. I sure hope a lot of people don't get hurt."

"I certainly hope and pray that's the case. And, by the way son, let's not tell your mother about this little talk. We wouldn't want to worry her about the current situation. This discussion is just between the men of the family."

In February 1848, the constitutional monarchy was overthrown. There were signs of discontent even though the nation had relative stability since 1840. Louis Philippe and his ministers prided themselves on their moderation and there was relative prosperity at home and peace abroad. However, the urban workers were mired in their misery and were increasingly drawn toward socialism.

Moreover, in 1846 a crop failure led to an economic crisis. Food became scarce and prices rose dramatically. Unemployment increased and many businesses failed. Within the government itself, high officials were involved in scandals and growing dissension. Novelists such as Victor Hugo, and George Sand glorified the common man as never before.

Beginning in 1847, opposition leaders set out to take full advantage of the restless atmosphere and to force the current regime to grant liberal reforms. Since political meetings were banned in public, they held a series of political "banquets" to mobilize the forces of discontent. This campaign was to be climaxed by a mammoth banquet in Paris in February, 1848. However the government, fearing violence, ordered the affair cancelled. On the 22nd, crowds of disgruntled students and unhappy workers gathered in the streets and began to clash with the police.

They hated Francois Guizot, who had emerged in 1840 as the key figure in the ministry, and the king expected no serious trouble. The weather was bad and a considerable army garrison was available if needed. But the disorders continued to spread, and the loyalty of the National Guard seemed to be questionable. After two days of rioting, Louis-Philippe made a choice to appease the demonstrators rather to create a bloodbath by unleashing the army. His announcement to replace Guizot as is chief minister came too late. By the morning of February 24, confronted by full scale civil war, he announced his abdication in favour of his nine year old grandson and fled to England.

The succession to the throne was not to be decided so quick and easily, however. Prior to an election in April, universal suffrage was proclaimed, increasing the electorate at a stroke from 200,000 to 9,000,000. By April 23, when Frenchmen went to the polls to elect their assembly, the initial mood of brotherhood had largely evaporated. Paris had become a caldron of political activism as dozens of factions sprung up.

The election returns confirmed the radicals' fears as the country voted overwhelmingly for conservative or moderate candidates. Radicals or socialists won only about 80 of the 880 seats available. Approximately 500 went to bourgeois republicans and about 300 to constitutional monarchists. When the assembly convened in May the new majority showed little caution or patience as they abolished the Luxembourg Commission and refused to substitute a better program of public works to provide for the unemployed. Thus the 'second republic' was born in turmoil.

The immediate consequence was a brief and bloody civil war in Paris-the so-called June Days (June 23-26, 1848). Thousands of workers suddenly cut off the state payroll were joined by students, artisans, and unemployed workers in a spontaneous protest movement. Barricades were erected in many working-class sections of the city. The biggest street war in the history of mankind was well underway.

As barricades go, the largest by far was the Saint-Antoine, measuring approximately seven hundred feet long and three stories high. The main components of this monster came from the ruins of three seven-story houses. Some said the balance of material included everything — even the kitchen sink. Pavement, stones, doors, pots, broken timber all contributed to the immensity of the barrier. Other barricades fanned out to the rear of the Saint-Antoine making the area quite a formidible fortification.

The barricades held on until the third and fourth days. The French assembly turned to Gen. Louis Gavaignac, who had made his mark repressing Algerian rebel tribes, and entrusted him with full powers to do the same in Paris. He brought in heavy artillery against the barricades and they finally fell.

At least 1,500 rebels were killed and more then 12,000 were arrested, many subsequently exiled in Algeria. The radical movement was stopped in it's tracks. The remaining students and workers withdrew into silent and bitter opposition.

A YOUNG CASUALTY

Early in rebellion Pierre Lacroix, a 14 year old lad living near the barricades, was summoned rather firmly by his mother. "Pierre, there's trouble in the streets, get to the market early for me today," said Madame Lacroix. "And take the long way around, there's been some shooting." "Whatever you say mama," was the untruthful reply of Pierre, who definitely wanted a closer look at the hostilities and of course the giant barricade.

"I'll be back in an hour, at most." He would be using the extra time to check out the scene rather than taking the prescribed longer route.

It was early on an overcast morning with some light fog hanging over the city. Pierre had been gone just over ten minutes as he neared one of the smaller barricades. He figured with a quick dash to some trees about 50 yards away a good vantage point to view Saint-Antoine could be gained. About half way toward his goal two shots rang out! Only one hitting its mark was needed to bring down the adventurous Pierre down. The ball had struck Pierre squarely between the hip and the knee shattering the large upper leg bone. In great pain he dragged himself past the trees and help at a nearby house.

Poor Pierre had been taken for an army spy by the rebels who were deadly serious about holding their barricades. They were definitely shooting first and asking questions later. Because of this incident Pierre's leg was amputated and his life changed forever.

During the recuperative period, Pierre had ample time to reflect on his life up to that point. Young as he was, Pierre seemed to mature and grow up rapidly after losing his leg near the barricade. He had not experienced a happy childhood, primarily because of alcoholic parents. Not that they were drunk all the time, but some of the weekends were very ugly. Arguments and bickering abounded and he hated to see his mother the object of physical abuse. The lumps on her head and the occasional black eye had an adverse effect on the young boy and he vowed never to allow these situations to develop later in life, when he had taken a wife. He firmly implanted into his subconscious a pledge of love and respect for some future spouse, whoever she may be.

Moreover, Pierre envisioned something of a plan, or perhaps it was more likely a dream, to finish his education and leave his current surroundings and become self-sufficient as soon as humanly possible. He realized long before leaving the hospital that his success would require diligence on his part and a lackadaisical attitude would most certainly condemn him to a lifetime of dependence on others and probably an inescapable situation in his current home. Thus Pierre became strong-willed and determined in his rehabilitation program, such as it was, and gave the extra effort necessary to propel him toward a positive future.

1851 - 71

For the residents of Paris, turmoil was far from over. In December, 1851, the arrest of seventy leading politicians led to several days of agitation. Barricades again went up in the streets as crowds clashed with police and troops. Several hundred demonstrators were killed and 27,000 arrested in Paris and in the provinces and surrounding areas.

By the following December, Napoleon III was proclaimed emperor of the French. The era which followed, 1852-1870 was known as the Second Empire. The period from 1852-59 was referred to as the authoritarian years. Civil liberties were narrowly prescribed; vocal opponents of the regime remained in exile or were compelled to remain silent. Parliament's activities were limited and elections were spaced at six-year intervals and were controlled by Napoleon's prefects, who sponsored official candidates.

The next period was called the liberal years. Napoleon's new foreign policy stirred up bitter controversy in France. Events during the next decade seemed to confirm warnings given by the emperor's advisors. The empire ran into increasingly stormy weather. Napoleon had become involved in diplomatic brinksmanship with Prussia's Bismarck, who had recorded victories recently over Denmark and Austria. In July, 1870, France was goaded into declaring war with Germany. The French armies were slow to mobilize and not yet ready to fight when the Prussian forces crossed into France. In September the Prussians won a decisive victory and Napoleon himself was taken prisoner. The regime could not survive such a humiliation. A subsequent revolution was the most bloodless in French history.

An armistice was signed in January 1871, and the terms were severe. France was charged a war indemnity of 5,000,000,000 francs, plus the cost of maintaining a German occupation army in eastern France until the indemnity was paid. Alsace and half of Lorraine were annexed to the new German empire. Also, the German army was authorized to stage a victory march through the Arc de Triomphe.

Paris was in an ugly mood from mid-March through May, climaxing with the "Bloody Week" (May 21-28). The 'communards' resisted, street by street, but were pushed back steadily to the heart of Paris. In their desperation, they executed a number of hostages, including the archbishop of Paris, and in the last days set fire to many public buildings. Twenty thousand communards were killed in the fighting or executed on the spot. Thousands of survivors were deported to the Penal Islands, while others escaped into exile.

JEAN'S ODYSSEY

In the Autumn of 1851, Jean Pontmercy joined a group of fifteen other boys in their mid-teens on a trip to the French Alps for hiking, camping and general nature studies which promised to be a great help in his education, especially in the disciplines of the sciences. Paul Lassalle was selected and hired as the leader of the excursion. He was an employee of the state and an experienced mountain climber and survival expert. Three of the boys' fathers joined the leader as counselors. Marius was not among them due to business commitments.

As the youth were divided into four teams, we will address the activities of Albert, Jules, Roger and, of course, Jean. Jule's father, Monsieur Cugnot, was in charge of the team which assumed the name 'Intrepid'. Due to the distance involved and the extended travel time, the expedition actually began in late summer and was scheduled to encompass slightly over four weeks. This endeavor was in the planning stages for quite some time and all of the boys were looking forward to an exciting time away from home.

Although funds were not a problem, Jean's major obstacle in making this trip was convincing his mother he was old enough and mature enough to spend so much time away from home and to be "roughing it" so to speak. Cosette's argument followed this line of reasoning, "Jean, you know your father is tied up with an important case. I would feel so much better if he was going along as one of the counselors." "But mother," Jean replied, "My best friends are going and one of their fathers will be our counselor." "Yes, I know Jean. Isn't it enough I'll be worried about you now, but in two years your sister will probably want to travel to England or somewhere else just to try to outdo you." "That may be true mother, but I can't be left out for such a reason. My friends would desert me, if I don't go on this trip." In the end, with almost whole-hearted support from Marius, permission was granted.

Fortunately, a major portion of the journey was made utilizing the blossoming railroad system which was just recently beginning to wind it's way throughout France. The destination was Mont Blanc, well over 200 miles to the southeast. With a peak stretching nearly 16,000 ft. into the heavens, Mont Blanc was truly an awesome sight to behold. It promised to be an inspiration and a challenge to the group of youths who represented some of the finest families in Paris.

Upon reaching the mountainous area, the campers were surprised to notice the leaves on some of the trees were already starting to change color. Despite travelling south the temperature was slightly cooler owing to the 2,500 ft. elevation of the lodge in which they were staying. The following day would find the group making their way to a cluster of cabins which would act as a base camp and were approximately 6,000 ft. above sea level.

At breakfast the next morning, Roger was the first to speak. "We're not going past the timberline today or any other day on this trip." "Oh really" Jules commented, "How high is that anyway?" "Around 11,500 ft. — give or take a few hundred feet" replied Roger. "What's the difference?" remarked Albert. "We'll do plenty of hiking and fish at a large lake in the area." "Listen Albert, we can fish and hike anywhere in France. Mont Blanc is over 15,000 ft. high and we should go above the timberline. Our team is the Intrepid — the fearless. We must accomplish something the others will not even dare to try. Let's go above the trees. Are we all together on this?" "How do you know it's not on the program", Jean wanted to know. "It's not on the schedule," Albert assured them. "I heard part of a conversation among the counselors last night." "I think we should give it a try," Jules said. The others agreed thus making the decision unanimous.

Two days after leaving the base camp the group reached the highest point on their agenda at approximately 9,500 ft. Each of the teams were accumulating merit points for setting up the camps properly and a variety of nature related subjects. These included tree and plant identification as well as bird and mammal awareness. However, the team Jean was aligned with discussed other plans when out of earshot of M. Cugnot, their counselor.

Roger, the self-proclaimed leader of the Intrepid team, began reviewing their totally unauthorized designs for the next day. "We will leave the main group one half hour before dawn and by the time the others get up we'll be over a mile away, heading up the north slope toward the timberline." "I have a short note written to let the counselors know the general area we're headed to and that our return will be before dark at the next scheduled camp site," Jean added. Jules nodded in agreement and remarked, "The weather seems much colder and damper today, doesn't it?" "Of course it does" Albert said, "Because of the high elevation." "Don't worry," Roger told them, "snow isn't expected in the area for at least two weeks yet."

The Intrepid team deliberately set up their tent a little farther from the rest of the group in order to better facilitate their stealthy getaway in the predawn darkness. They were well underway before the others realized what had transpired. Unknown to them, they were assessed a penalty of 100 points for their audacious side trip. The penalty dropped them into last place with little hope of bettering their position.

As the first rays of light teased the eastern sky, Jean said to the others "That was easier than I thought it would be. We were careful and we were very quiet." "They must have been very tired from the previous day," Jules added. "I thought at least one person would have heard something," Albert said. "Let's concentrate on our goals for today," Roger reminded them. "We have to cover about twice as much ground as the others in order to reach the next campsite before dark."

They moved along quickly and crossed the timberline by eleven o'clock. Roger pushed them upward for another hour before stopping for their lunch break. Jules was the first to notice a change in the weather. "The wind is really picking up and the sky getting darker all the time. We should leave here soon and go to the camp site." "Don't be in such a hurry, friends. Enjoy the view -- This may be the only time any of us are able to climb to this altitude," Roger implored them.

The view was indeed becoming obscured with each passing minute. A fast moving cold front from the north was bearing rapidly down on them as they prepared to move on. Although feeling cold the youths were hardly aware of the actual temperature. They naively assumed the dark clouds fast approaching were a quickly passing snow squall or perhaps a heavy rain shower. How wrong they were! Before they had covered a hundred yards Albert exclaimed "Well, our first snowfall of the year. This will pass quickly, Roger, isn't that so?" "Of course it will. Just keep moving along. We don't reach the southbound trail for about three miles." "Three miles" Jules groaned. "Stop complaining boys," Roger chided them. Jean, who was last in the single file group as Roger led, remarked, "The snow is much heavier now. This may not be a sudden squall as we first thought."

After a half hour passed the trail was covered with an inch of snow. The south trail would be harder to spot as time went by. It was not possible to just descend the slope at any given break in the landscape, for boulders or trees below could virtually seal it off and triple their time needed to reach the next campsite.

The snow continued to intensify and as Roger spoke, Jean noticed a note of concern in his voice. "There's a fork in the trail ahead. We should take the lower trail. It appears to be a short cut." "Let's take it," Jules and Albert said in unison. Jean tried to overrule them but he was outnumbered three to one. The new trail quickly led them back to the timberline but then the terrain grew considerably rougher and harder to pass. They walked on and on, until it became obvious to all that they were making a wide circle and getting nowhere. Roger was now snapping at Jules and Albert whenever they opened their mouths. Worst of all, he was devoid of any new ideas to remove the group from the winter-like weather they were enduring for the past several hours. In short, he was losing his place as the leader of the team.

When the snow reached the main party the younger ones were ecstatic with the realization they were experiencing one of the earliest snowfalls in memory for that area. However, the counselors were very uneasy about the white blanket that was descending upon them. The boys who decided to leave for the higher trails could be in real trouble. Mont Blanc possessed a peak that was continually capped with snow, but snow at this altitude in early September was unusual indeed. By the early afternoon M. Lassalle, the expedition leader, set a plan in motion.

"One team will return to our campsite of last night in case they return. Another team will continue on to our original destination and I will take the remaining team along with M. Cugnot and ascend the south trail. We will have enough personnel to split into two smaller groups if the need arises. Are there any questions?" There were none from the now serious group of campers.

When darkness was approaching the wayward team, Jean asserted himself by remarking "We're losing daylight rapidly and it's not likely we'll find the south trail today. With about six inches of snow on the ground we should make camp at the next favorable site we come to." Roger mumbled softly to himself but said nothing. "We don't have much to eat," complained Albert. "That's right" said Jules, "We were planning to have supper at a large campsite with all the others." "Let's just get this tent up and build a fire as soon as we can" stated a very cold and wet Albert.

Jean distributed the leftovers from the noon meal that seemed to have occurred so long ago. The small amount of dried fruit in their possession would serve as breakfast in the morning. Luckily there was an ample supply of tea at their disposal and an endless supply of water for boiling, thanks to the heavy snowfall. Speaking of snow, it was still falling steadily although not as heavy as earlier in the day. Their camp was well selected near some large boulders and a stand of evergreens. The covering of pine needles was merged with only about an inch of finely sifted snow. However, the temperature was destined to drop almost 15 degrees lower than anything they had experienced since their travels began.

Paul Lassalle was a rugged individualist. Eldest of five children, he preferred to live alone. Not that he was home that much. He worked on a fishing boat when he was old enough to leave the rest of his family. Later he became an expert hunter and led hunting trips in various areas. He enjoyed mountain climbing and earned part of his living as a guide for expeditions such as the one he was involved with at the present time. Most trips went smoothly, although he had witnessed a sprinkling of accidents, lost campers and weather related problems. But even Paul, with nearly 20 years of the outdoor lifestyle, hadn't seen winter arrive so early in these mountains.

M. Cugnot arose just after Paul and found almost four inches of snow on the ground. They both knew this accumulation could be translated into eight to twelve inches in the higher elevations. The youths were roused from their bedding and all consumed a hasty breakfast. There was much ground to cover and time was becoming more important in uniting the entire group.

Two thousand feet higher Jean was the first to greet the cold white morning. "Everyone up! We need to start a fire quickly." The others began stirring and soon a fire was blazing and water for tea was heating. As they were making preparations to get underway, Jules asked "What are our plans for this morning?" Jean had thought long and hard about that subject before falling asleep the previous night and answered, "As the terrain allows, we're going to take a diagonal line of descent toward the south trail. By that method we will be headed in the right direction toward last nights intended campsite and also should see a lighter amount of snow depth as we travel." "I agree," added Roger, who seemed in better spirits now that the snow had stopped. In their partially sheltered camp area they saw about three inches of finely sifted snow grow to 12" in the open area with some higher drifts.

The four took turns leading and breaking the trail, so to speak. The others, including Roger, looked to Jean now, whenever they needed an answer or some clear judgement on an issue. After an hour or so into their trek, Roger was out in front when he exclaimed, "There's a small creek up ahead, let's check it out." They encountered a stream about 20 feet wide and it appeared to be fairly shallow. Roger noticed a fallen tree 25 yards downstream and made his way toward it. The tree completely spanned the creek and was about eight feet above the water due to high embankments.

"We can save time by walking over on the trunk of this tree," Roger told the others. "He's right," Albert said. "We could lose an hour or more looking for a place to cross and we would get too wet trying to wade over to the other side," Jules commented. "Hold on a minute friends," Jean said. But it was too late. Roger was on the fallen tree and starting across. The powdery snow floated toward the water below with each step he took. When he reached the middle Roger said, "This is easy, just take your time." Suddenly with his next step he encountered some ice under the snow and slipped off the tree trunk despite flailing efforts to grab the trunk with his hands. With a loud splash he landed in three feet of frigid water. While the water was not deep enough to drown in, it was also not deep enough to break his fall sufficiently. With an outcry of pain he scrambled to the embankment from which he had departed and it was soon obvious to all that he had fractured his right ankle.

Jean said to Albert and Jules "start a fire as fast as possible. We must get him warm and dry out his clothes." Roger was trembling with cold as Jean checked his ankle and was relieved to learn it was not a compound fracture. Jules busied himself clearing an area for the fire and a spot where Roger could try to make himself comfortable. Albert soon had enough wood to get a roaring fire going. They were fortunate to be slightly below the timberline where wood was available.

Roger's wet clothing was stripped off and he was temporarily covered with two of their overnight blankets. When Jean asked him how he felt, Roger replied, "The chills are almost gone and surprisingly the ankle doesn't feel too bad without weight on it. As soon as I get a change of clothes on, we should leave." The idea of constructing a makeshift litter was rejected by Jean, who told the others, "We will take turns helping Roger along and travel two by two. The front pair will break the trail and the pair in the rear, including Roger, will follow closely behind. As we travel mostly downhill the depth of the snow should begin to diminish in the lower altitudes." What do you think the others are doing now?" Jules wanted to know. "We can't tell for sure," Jean replied, "but I think they'll stay at their present site another day before they start searching."

The search party of six, headed by Paul and M. Cugnot, was at this point less than two miles from the Intrepid team. The main problem was that distance was now lengthening — not getting shorter. By passing the point of intersection via the "short cut", the searchers were still heading due north to higher altitudes and the place of intersection with the main east-west trail. Paul said to M. Cugnot and the four youths "We're making good progress. We may split up when we reach the main trail to the north." M. Cugnot, who was now concerned about his son Jules, remarked "I really hope we locate the lads before another night falls. They can take care of themselves pretty well but I'm sure they wouldn't delay this expedition unless they were lost or had other problems." "I'm confident they're alright," Paul assured them, "That heavy snow probably has them disoriented." The group trekked on into the early afternoon.

"I've got to rest for awhile. My foot is throbbing worse than before," Roger stated with pain interwoven through each word. "Another fifty yards to that thicket up ahead," Jean told him. He also said to Albert, "Go back and help Jules with him. The snow isn't very deep anymore and its not a problem to get through." They took a lengthy break and built another fire to keep Roger warm as he rested. Jean now revised their plans for the rest of the day. "We'll make camp for the night at the intersection with the south trail. That's less than two miles from here. Tomorrow we can reach the lower campsite with Roger better rested. I'm sure there will be at least one team there, even if some are searching." No words of protest were heard from the others. Two hours later camp was made and a meager supper of hot tea and some broken cookies was gulped. The remaining dried fruit would be consumed in the morning leaving only a few rations of tea in their possession.

Upon reaching the east-west trail, Paul decided to split the group. He would take two of the boys and travel west in the direction the missing team would be coming from and M. Cugnot would go east and look for signs the lost team had taken that path. Their two small groups agreed to travel one hour and then double back and look for a good place to spend the night after they rejoined.

After a fruitless hour with no sign of anyone in their respective areas the mini teams regrouped again and prepared to set up camp. About 10 minutes after two of the youths were sent out to gather wood there was a crashing sound heard out in the brush -- and then a cry for help.

"A bear is chasing us" cried Richard, one of the boys who were sent. Paul grabbed a flaming branch from the newly started fire and held it up. He said to the others, "Keep working on that fire." About 30 yards away a female black bear emerged with two cubs born the previous spring. She pushed the cubs back and came slowly forward emitting some ferocious growls. Paul picked up another branch and told the others to be still on the opposite side of the fire. The angry bear came within ten yards and rose up on her hind legs and growled some and waved her forepaws menacingly but came no closer. Soon the crisis was over as the bears disappeared over a hill in the distance.

Early the following morning the Intrepid team started down the south trail. Roger's ankle was in need of medical attention and all were in need of food and fresh water. Jean tried to encourage the others as they made their way slowly down the mountain, taking turns assisting Roger "It's not much further friends. We'll soon be at a large campsite with provisions and I'm sure at least one of the other teams will be there as well. Then, in one more day the end of our journey at a fair sized town with a doctor for Roger's ankle. The rest of the group liked those words and moved on with hope and determination.

When they finally reached their destination there were actually two teams there as the rear guard team moved ahead after spending a day of waiting with no avail. They soon enjoyed a good meal and made Roger as comfortable as possible. Before long the main search team was on the scene as they had seen nothing on the trails they were on. There would be some stern lectures and reprimands forthcoming but for now their main course of action was the medical attention for Roger's ankle and the completion of their trip, which was already three days behind schedule.

After reaching home the following week, Jean was warmly greeted by his parents and sister Ponine. Of course Marius and Cosette wanted to know each and every detail and Jean never tired of going over the story completely. Even Ponine did not get on his nerves as she did sometimes. In fact, Jean was so glad to return home he gave his sister the largest and longest hug they both could remember.

ALEXANDRE-GUSTAVE EIFFEL

As we have moved ahead through the corridors of time, let us once again retreat to the past. Not the far distant past, but we will return briefly to 1832, that mystical yet devastating, hopeful although brutal year of turmoil. A year that brought more than it's share of death, also ushered in life toward the end of the year in the east-central city of Dijon.

Born December 15, 1832, Alexandre-Gustave Eiffel went on to become a bridge engineer, graduating from the Ecole Centrale des Arts et Manufacturers in 1855. He specialized in metal construction, especially bridges. He directed the erection of an iron bridge at Bordeaux in 1858, followed by several others, and designed the lofty, arched Galerie des Machines for the Paris exhibition of 1867.

His 540-foot (162-metre) span Garabit Viaduct over the Truyere in southern France was, for many years, the highest bridge in the world. It towered 400 feet (120 metres) over the stream. And still, despite these major accomplishments, the best was yet to come.

The city of Dijon, located approximately 200 miles southeast of Paris by road, has many outstanding old buildings, some dating back to the 15th century. It is situated near a plain of fertile vineyards and at the confluence of the Ouche and Suzon rivers.

Dijon was most prosperous in the 18th century, when it was an intellectual centre of France. The city declined after the French Revolution when its provincial institutions were suppressed. However, the coming of the railways in 1851 brought it new wealth, and the population began a long tradition of continued growth.

The university, founded in 1722, has faculties of law, science and letters, as well as a medical school. The city has been a diocese since 1731. The buildings of the palace of the Dukes of Burgundy are located in the centre of the old city. The original medieval palace was largely rebuilt and extended in the 17th and 18th centuries.

And so, this was the area in which Alexandre-Gustave, a very gifted and talented young man, lived and grew and was educated and built marvelous structures.

Then said He unto them, nation shall rise against nation, and kingdom against kingdom.

Luke 21:10

Chapter V

FRANCINE

. . . .

AN ENTERPRISING FAMILY

Charles and Isabelle Aigner were married in 1829 after a brief courtship. Actually they had known and admired one another for the previous five years but romance bloomed rather suddenly. Clothing and fashions in general commanded so much of their time, little else was possible. He had been born into a couturiere way of life whereas she had selected it based on her ambitions and desires. For years it could have been said that these two well matched persons were hardly ever seen without a pair of scissors or a pattern in their hands.

After a stillbirth in 1831, Victor was born 15 months later. Daughters Francine and Lucile were born in 1836 and 1840 respectively. Another son, Jerome, was born in 1842 but succumbed to pneumonia before entering school. The devastated family only became more deeply engrossed in their work than before. The other children flourished and, as time went by, it was observed that Francine had a better head for business than Victor.

During the insurrection and rioting of 1848 it should be mentioned that a group of rebels on the run from the National Guard found refuge in the Aigners clothing factory which was closed at the time. This unnamed gang of eight were among the rowdiest of the protesters and seemed to be taking part only for the sake of mayhem and chaos without any distinct causes or agendas.

With the crisis at hand, the bunch remained silent for two hours and finally began to grow restless.

Rebel No. 1 said to Rebel No. 2, "Wait, I know this place. I worked here three summers ago - until I was discharged."

No. 2 queried, "What was a fine fellow like you fired for?"

"A minor infraction at most, pinching."

"Now No. 1 what or who did you pinch?"

"Only a few, No. 2, only a few."

"A few what, No. 1?"

"A few of my co-workers, that's all No. 2"

"Oh."

"You see No. 2, over the summer many young women from the university are hired as temporaries."

"So."

"Well No. 2, it was a very warm summer and those Aigners, they didn't hire many of the poor plain women. They took the best of the university lovelies and with the heat as it was the petticoat layer was, shall we say, at a bare minimum."

"I'm beginning to see, No. 1."

"Precisely, No. 2. You see, the way they bent over their cutting tables and I had so many trips to make up and down those narrow aisles, what choice did I have. They had no chairs and only sat during their dinner break."

"Tell me more No. 1."

"Not much more to tell No. 2. Being right handed I naturally threw the bolts of material over my left arm and walked down the aisles and threw a pinch here and there. Most of them didn't mind. The ones that did straightened up before I passed by."

"Who squealed No. 1?"

"A fairly new hire. Very straight laced compared to the rest. She didn't know my methods and was quite upset and I got the gate."

"With no references I'm sure," added No. 2.

"No comment," replied No. 1, as the conversation ended with the sound of approaching footsteps.

Rebels No. 3 and 4 were returning after casing the factory for anything edible. It seems the balance of the group was catching up on their rest.

No. 3 announced, "There's precious little to eat in this place, unless you're a moth."

"Correct," No. I replied. "But before we leave this place after dark we'll leave our calling card."

"And what will that be?" No. 2 asked.

"For firing me that summer we will show them how much damage eight pair of scissors can do in an hour."

Besides cutting up many years of expensive fabric, the rebels discovered some jars of dye and inflicted more damage with those substances than with the scissors. They probably would have torched the building but chose not to attract attention to themselves.

Less than two years after the loss of their son, the Aigners had to recover from a heavily vandalized factory. Not to be deterred, the family rolled up their sleeves and worked even harder than before. Despite their efforts it took nearly a year to recover their losses and bring operations back to normal. The fact was the business far exceeded all past records and by the early fifties was among the top two or three in Paris in their field of endeavor.

In the summer of 1851 a seemingly carefree outing almost provided the chance for tragedy to again strike the Aigner family. A balmy weekend afternoon found the family at a park where the more opulent residents of the city gathered in warm weather. The area provided numerous picnic areas and many flat grassy sections for croquet or similar activities. But it was the shallow lake and the opportunity to go boating that was the villain of the scenario.

Becoming bored on Terra Firma, Lucile and Francine pleaded to paddle the lake in one of the boats which were available to all for a small rental fee. The parents agreed with the admonition to stay close to the shore. They naturally agreed and began paddling in a small arc and then reversed the process. The arc gradually grew wider and soon approached the rope used to cordon off the shallow area from the deeper section.

Due to heavier than average rains the week before, the shallows were almost a foot higher than usual and the deep part had risen even more. The girls hadn't noticed but the gentle summer breeze had freshened during the past hour and they certainly did not have a clue as to the weakness of the frayed cordon rope which had been in use for several seasons at that point. A larger gust of wind struck at the apex of their arc pushed their small boat through the cordoned area and into the central part of the lake.

It happened that Francine was an adequate swimmer but Lucile, although somewhat fascinated with boats and large ships, had a disdain for water other than what was drawn for her own bath. Awful imaginations coursed through her mind when the cordon snapped and she began screaming. The boat commenced rocking and as Francine attempted to comfort her the craft capsized. With a little effort Francine could touch the bottom of the lake with her toes, while holding on to the side of the boat. Lucile, however, only 11 and four or five inches shorter did not have that luxury. She looked around desperately for Lucile but she was nowhere to be seen.

In reality Lucile was flung out of reach of the boat on the opposite side. Her head plunged below the surface and had not reappeared.

"Help!" Francine screamed as she turned toward her family on shore.

An instant later Charles and Victor understood the situation perfectly and ran for the nearest boat.

"Hold on girls!" Charles yelled across the lake.

He spoke in plural - even though he saw only one of his daughters. Victor pushed the back of the boat into the water and both paddled furiously.

A large splash occurred about 15 feet from Francine as Lucile's head broke through the surface of the water. A half scream mingled with a huge gasp for air as Lucile thrashed the water with both arms. Seeing her sister going under again, Francine left the safety of the overturned boat and swam toward her. They were about 75 yards from the shore where they had departed earlier.

By this time Charles and Victor had traveled half the distance to the distressed girls. They were now shouting encouragement.

"Hurry Francine - hold her up. Don't let her go under again!"

Francine reached her sister just in time as her head almost disappeared and she swallowed more of the lake water. Lucile was still thrashing wildly but Francine managed to hold her up until help arrived. It remains extremely doubtful whether she could have completed the rescue herself, all the way back to the shore.

After pulling the girls into the boat, Lucile coughed and sputtered all the way back to the stoney beach area. A very anxious Isabelle was not fully relieved until all four were on dry ground.

Lucile's first coherent sentence was "Now I hate boats too. I'll never set foot in one again." The family, very thankful and happy with the outcome, just hugged Lucile and smiled but said nothing. Needless to report the episode terminated their outing for the afternoon and the family returned home somewhat in awe over the fragility of life.

In 1853 the Aigners repeated a success they had realized in 1847 with an award winning spring collection of their fashion line. The year 1850 produced similar results for their fall couture line. The family had indeed established itself firmly in the elite inner circle of Paris fashions. Life was proving enjoyable and rewarding when hard work and dedication were applied with love and fairness. However the children were maturing and changes mingled with new challenges and dangers loomed ahead as the decade approached the mid point.

A LABOR OF LOVE

Jean Pontmercy was in his third year at the University of Paris and he was in love. The year was 1855. The woman was Francine Aigner. Francine was graceful as a gentle breeze, sophisticated yet friendly, possessing chestnut brown hair with reddish highlights and hazel eyes that were as mysterious as they were beautiful. And, with her family on the cutting edge of high fashion in Paris, she always seemed to be wearing something exquisite, with each outfit more beautiful than the last.

The main problem that existed was that Jean was far from alone in his captivation with Francine. Others adored her. She already had three offers for marriage and Jean was hesitant to make it four. She was not being courted by anyone special at the time and usually had a different escort for each social she attended. These admirers were just so completely dazzled that they offered her their hearts on the slim chance she may accept.

Whenever Jean felt that his quest for her love was hopeless, he walked the streets in her neighborhood late in the evening. This had worked for him twice before, why not again. His spirits seemed to be lifted just knowing that in one certain very large residence dwelt an angel. When he returned to his dormitory quarters his head was clear and he fared well the next day in his studies.

This particular evening began like the others. He had a bite to eat at his favorite pub around ten and started walking. "Good evening Monsieur, nice weather we're having," said Henri the officer walking his beat. "Good evening to you, Henri. Seems to be a very quiet evening at that." Henri's beat included the University area and was probably the only officer Jean knew on a first name basis. "Let's hope it stays that way, nice and quiet," returned the officer as their paths parted.

Jean passed the angel's habitat and circled for his return trip. As usual, the house was dark as all had retired for the night. Or had they? Was that a small light on the first floor, he wondered. Jean stopped and looked again. The light was not constant, it was getting brighter. That light was not a light — It was a fire.

At first Jean couldn't believe his eyes, then he swung into action. The large home was set back from the street about one hundred feet and had a fence and gate. He quickly passed through the gate and raced toward the house. In a flash he was up the porch steps and hammering his fists on the front door, as he cried out "Fire. Fire!"

For a period of time that seemed like an eternity, there was no response. Then, after what was actually only about a scant minute or two, stirring of people inside began. The house contained twelve rooms and was inhabited by eight persons which included two servants. Jean knew Francine had an older brother and a younger sister, and her parents and maternal grandmother were there as well.

After a few moments people began leaving by the side door onto the porch and the front door where Jean was standing. They came out coughing and sputtering. There was extensive smoke present although no one seemed to have suffered any burns as of yet. The fire by now was spreading from the kitchen area through portions of the first floor, with only Victor, Francine's brother, trying to quell its progress.

M. Aigner said to a neighbor who had arrived on the scene, "Please go for help. We have a serious fire here." The neighbor obeyed. "Everyone gather here on the porch, we must account for all family members," added the head of the household. Jean had seen the servants and Lucile, the youngest of the children, but as of then had not seen Francine. He raced around the house, checking the back door and the yard. When he returned to the front, Victor stumbled outside gasping for air. "It's becoming hopeless unless help arrives with volunteer fire fighters with buckets and other equipment."

"Where is Francine?" Jean interrupted with a loud voice. "Oh dear," M. Aigner sighed, "Everyone's here but Francine. Her bedroom is on the third floor. I must go back in for my eldest daughter." He was restrained by Victor and a neighbor. "We need a tall ladder, that's the only way now," Victor commented.

Just then a blood-curdling scream was heard from inside, "Help! Please help me!" It was Francine. Jean took immediate action. He grabbed a quilt which was hanging over the porch railing and burst in through the front door. Luckily the stairway was located in the front part of the house and was illuminated by the flames. The heat was intense but the smoke was probably less than earlier when the fire was merely in a smouldering stage.

The steps to the third floor were much smokier again. Jean began calling, "Francine, Francine, where are you? I need to hear your voice in this heavy smoke." "Over here, hurry" came the reply. It was easy to see how she was disoriented and couldn't find her way out in this smokey inferno. Jeans hair was singed and his feet felt like they were on fire themselves.

Suddenly he bumped into something in the hallway. It was Francine trying to crawl to safety. "Francine, it's Jean my love, I'm here for you." "Jean Pontmercy, is that really you?" Francine gasped as she passed out. He gathered her up in his arms and headed down the staircase. Upon reaching the hottest area below the second floor landing he flipped the quilt down over Francine to protect her face and hair. Jean leaped through the searing heat and flames with his precious cargo being his main concern and himself secondary. After charging down off the porch he placed Francine down by her waiting parents and blacked out himself amid the sounds of cheering by the crowd which had accumulated because of the fire.

By the time the blaze was under control the house sustained considerable damage, but at least it was repairable. Fortunately the Aigners affluence easily permitted a sizeable country cottage that could meet their needs for an extended period of time. There was even a detached bungalow for use as servants' quarters.

As for the pair that had been in such deadly peril, Francine fared much the better. She suffered mainly from smoke inhalation and a couple of minor burns on her feet that blistered slightly. Jean, on the other hand, lost approximately fifty per cent of his hair and had second degree burns on his hands and ankles. Luckily they were not severed enough as to cause permanent scarring, just painful and compelled him to spend a few days in the hospital.

Francine, who visited him daily during his brief stay, asked Jean the following question during one of the visits, "How did you happen to be in the area that evening?"

This question was the opening Jean needed to express his feelings for her and he replied, "Francine, I've been a secret admirer of yours for many months now. From the first day I saw you last semester, I knew I'd never see a more beautiful woman, even if I lived a hundred years. I saw you almost daily at the university and became totally convinced you had to be the best dressed person in all of Paris. Of course I noticed your 'following' of male admirers, men from important and respected families in Paris and elsewhere. What chance did I have? I could only hope and pray. The first time I saw you up close on a bright sunny day I was totally captivated by your eyes. So piercing, yet inquisitive, I almost tripped down the steps which were just ahead. Later on, whenever I had a really dismal day, I took to walking in your neighborhood, right by your house in fact and your mere presence behind those walls worked wonders for me. The night of the fire I almost walked by without noticing, but, you know the rest anyway. Oh, I'm probably boring you with my babbling."

"Not at all Jean. I had no idea you felt this way. I'm really quite enthralled by your heroism and now your apparent devotion. However, you must know I've promised my parents not to make any romantic commitments until after graduating from the university next year. I'm very interested in the fashion industry and they want me to take over the family business some day as Victor has shown little interest, if any."

"I understand," said Jean, somewhat disheartened. "May I see you socially in the near future, after I've fully recovered of course?"

"Certainly, now that you know my circumstances Jean, I'd be delighted. But for now, get well soon and keep in mind, and I'm being completely honest and sincere when I say this, I undoubtedly owe you my life, but I don't owe you my love, at least not for now."

Jean was entirely speechless with this revelation and adjusted his pillow rather clumsily.

As Francine rose to leave she added, "There is a young man I have special feelings for, Louis Danton, perhaps you are acquainted with him at the university."

"THE WOMANIZER"

Louis Danton. Of all people, the biggest cad in the university. Jean wondered to himself, how could a marvelous visit with Francine end like this. If it were only someone else the impact would be much easier to handle. This unbearable womanizer had broken more than one heart already, didn't Francine know about that suave operator.

In all actuality, Louis had broken three hearts during his stay at the university. Now in his fifth year in a four year program, he targeted the younger incoming female students. The younger, prettier, and wealthier ones were the types that peaked his interest. His plan of action included surveying the field in Autumn, making a selection to keep him warm during the cold nights in winter, and then gradually severing all ties by the time May flowers were in bloom.

Francine was Louis's leading candidate the previous year but he grew impatient with her devotion to her parents wishes and he sought, and found greener pastures. Still, he knew he had to try again this semester. Louis wanted her and looked at the opportunity as a challenge unlike any he had experienced since the onset of puberty. This time his plan was broader and more complex. This time he could be more patient and understanding with Francine. The reason for his increased optimism this year was

Monique, an outlet for current passions while the real prize held him at bay.

Danton, a man of average height; slightly above average looks; above average funds at his disposal, and an ego the size of the Matterhorn, met Monique at a local club. Monique Saucier, not a prostitute by any means, but an easy companion for a man of means with a smooth sales pitch. Someone who could easily be pictured as a part-time maid who needs very few days to seduce the wealthy, but unhappy, man of the house. Louis and Monique figured to be a perfect combination.

After Jean left the hospital and returned to the university he spoke with Francine on a daily basis. One day shortly after his return she inquired, "Jean, would you consider being our guest for dinner this Friday. My parents want to know more about you and also extend their gratitude for your heroic actions last month?"

"Why, yes of course. How considerate of them. I wasn't planning to go home this weekend anyway. What time shall I arrive?" "Dinner will be served at 7:00 but we would all like to see you around 6:00 to get better acquainted."

"Fine, it's settled then for 6:00 PM. I'm looking forward to meeting everyone under circumstances less trying. By the way I've never seen your summer home either."

The week seemed to drag very slowly for Jean. He was anxious to make a good impression on the parents, as Francine seemed to lean heavily on their advice. After all, he was studying to be a lawyer and hoped to follow in his father's footsteps, so to speak. This could be an evening destined to make or break his budding relationship with the epitome of womanhood.

When Friday finally arrived, Jean found that he was a bit nervous. Just relax, he thought to himself, I must be myself and not attempt complete perfection. "Come right in," said Victor Aigner in response to Jean's knock. "Thank you. This is an elegant place for a summer home, very roomy as well."

"We like it real well, Pontmercy." Victor had a habit of calling his male acquaintances by their last names. As M. Aigner entered the foyer he saw their guest had arrived. "Oh, there you are Jean, come in the sitting room and meet my wife and mother-in-law."

The remainder of the first hour was spent in the sitting room with Jean answering countless questions about his recovery from the burns and his family background and future plans. Victor seemed slightly annoyed at times with all the attention showered on their guest. Jean learned afterwards that the Aigners were not too receptive to Victor's request for a similar dinner with a female companion of somewhat questionable morals and upbringing.

As for the dinner, the main course was pheasant with all the trimmings and was enjoyed by all. Francine had arrived home late and joined the group just minutes before dinner began. "I had trouble finding transportation after leaving school later than usual," she explained. "Dessert will be served a little later, Jean, I'm sure we're all quite full now," commented Mme. Aigner. "Francine, why don't you and Lucile show Jean around the grounds. It's a nice evening for a walk," she continued.

The evening progressed wonderfully, as far as Jean was concerned, although Francine seemed a bit preoccupied from time to time. He was sure he had made a good impression with Francine's parents, although there seemed to be no detectable progress in the relationship with his hearts desire. What could be on her mind, Jean wondered. He hoped to find out soon without becoming too inquisitive or pushy.

Uppermost on Francine's agenda, and ranking second only to breathing, was the handling of a new dilemma which she faced. Along with her growing affection for Jean, she was offered an engagement by none other than Louis Danton. It was an offer carefully orchestrated not to cause parental objection. Louis would wait until the September after graduation for marriage, but wanted her promise now. He was desperately trying to convince Francine that he had become a changed man and stories she may have heard were probably greatly exaggerated.

Francine decided to petition Louis for an extension regarding her decision, especially after the dinner visit with Jean. Since Louis kept an apartment only a block from the university, she would just drop in after her last class of the day. Francine had no way of knowing that Louis had skipped his classes 'again' that particular day. He had a very good reason.

The apartment was on the second floor and Francine made her way surmising Louis would surely understand. After all, he was a changed man, wasn't he? On reaching the door, she found it to be slightly ajar. That's strange she thought as she was about to knock. The knock was halted in mid air as Francine heard someone giggling in the apartment. She paused, and then heard it again, along with raucous laughter easily recognizable as Louis's.

Francine stepped into the apartment without bothering to finish knocking. Moving through the living area she proceeded to the bathroom, the source of the giggling and, much to her dismay, a great deal of splashing. Once in the bathroom, Francine took in the whole picture in a glance. "Having fun Louis?" she inquired. Although he was, immensely, he was in no position to admit it. He just stammered, "I wasn't expecting you Francine. Uh, how did you get in anyway?"

"It doesn't matter, you ogre. How could you, after what we talked about?" she continued. "And who's this, Monique Saucier, tramp of the month." Francine recognized her amid the bubbles in the tub. She also took note of Monique's anatomical features which drew such interest from the opposite sex.

"Give me a chance to explain," pleaded Louis without much optimism in his voice. "Not likely. We're through Louis Danton! Why don't you propose to this slut?"

Francine, having finished her searing piece, strode over toward the tub, as Monique sat there wide-eyed in shocked amazement. She lifted a soapy sponge out of the water and in one motion swatted Monique smartly across the face. The recipient of the blow let out a shriek and began rubbing her eyes and Louis made no attempt to interfere. Francine then marched out of the apartment with an indignant look on her face.

During the next two weeks Jean saw very little of Francine on the grounds of the university. When their paths did intersect, she appeared to be quite busy and had precious little to say. It seemed to Jean she was heartsick and hurt about something. He hoped it was not he, who had offended her. In fact Jean would have given his last possession to comfort her and hold her in his arms just for a few minutes. He honestly felt deep within his own heart that he alone was capable of removing any hurt, of soothing any grief that beset that precious angel.

The next day Jean was rather nonchalantly handed a note by one of his friends. He saw at a glance it was written by a member of the opposite sex and opened it immediately. It was indeed from 'her' and he traced the lines of Francines penmanship over in his mind. The note itself, although beautiful to Jean, simply said, 'Please come this evening. I have something to discuss with you. We have returned to the main residence as repairs were completed. Francine.'

There was no mention of his expected arrival time, so Jean planned to arrive shortly after their normal dinner hour had passed. As Jean entered the gate and was walking toward the house he notice Victor sitting on the porch. "Pontmercy, what brings you over here tonight, as if I didn't know?" The thought crossed Jean's mind to call Victor by his last name as well, but he decided against it. "Evening, Victor. Is Francine in the house?" "Indeed she is. I'll get her and vacate the porch at the same time."

"That's good of you Victor. It appears we will need a bit of privacy this evening." Several minutes later Francine arrived on the porch. Jean had to admit, when he saw her, that she never looked more casual. At the university and the night of the dinner visit she was completely dressed up.

"Good evening Jean. It was good of you to come on short notice. "Good evening Francine. You look lovely tonight," Jean fibbed in reply.

"I really look terrible and my hair is a mess, but you wouldn't tell me that anyway, would you Jean."

"No, I don't think I would. You always look beautiful to me, Francine." "That's sweet of you to say that. But, let me tell you the main reason I asked you to come over this evening. Louis and I won't be seeing each other anymore. I wish somebody would have warned me about him. I'm tired of his type. Most men have only one thing on their minds. I don't think you're that type, are you Jean?" Jean cleared his throat and shifted his feet nervously and fibbed again slightly, "No, I don't consider myself a womanizer like Louis and some others. Although you certainly possess everything a man could want in a woman. There are, in my opinion, some activities that can wait until after marriage."

"I was hoping you'd feel that way, Jean. From this night on, I'm not seeking or accepting any new relationships with other men, providing you can make that same commitment about women in your life. "As God is my witness, I certainly can, Francine."

"You understand, I can't accept a formal engagement at this time, but I think we can have an agreement between the two of us."

"That's an agreement I can live with for as long as necessary. It's really no great sacrifice to be with the person I've loved for many months."

"I feel greatly relieved after sharing our feelings this evening, Jean. Now, if you don't mind, I'll be going in the house. I haven't slept well lately, but I think I will tonight."

"Good night Francine. I know I won't forget this night for as long as I live."

FRANCINE STALKED

Interest in Monique declined rapidly for Louis Danton after the embarrassing incident in his apartment. He wasn't accustomed to being the loser in a confrontation. With Francine he had, in effect, been a two-time loser over an eighteen month period of time, and it bothered him. The uppity female should not be allowed to humiliate him and get away with it. Louis planned to get her friendship back or make her pay a price she would remember.

The following week Jean noticed only a slight change in his relationship with Francine. He had apparently only regained the lost ground of the past couple of weeks. Knowing that didn't bother him too much as he could now be more patient and understanding. The next time he saw Francine, he was troubled when she said, "Jean, I think there may be a problem with Louis." "Louis Danton? What's he up to now?"

"I don't know. I'm just seeing too much of him around the university, and he always has something obnoxious to say. "Is that right, doesn't he know when to give up?" "I guess not, although I've made it very plain to him."

"I'll try to spend more time walking with you between classes. I'm interested in his reaction when he sees us together."

The couple had only to wait until the following day to find out. Early in the afternoon there was Louis waiting for Francine.

"Who's your new friend, Francine? Aren't I good enough for you anymore?"

"Where's your old friend, Monique? Did she leave you too, Louis?"

"That's none of your business, but if you must know, I got rid of her." Jean noticed that Louis had been drinking. Taking Francine by the arm, he ushered her away. "Leaving so soon. Hey Pontmercy, I heard you rescued the little lady. Good for you."

They continued to hear Louis babbling until they were out of earshot.

"Please let me know if he tries to get physical with you or hurts you in any way," Jean instructed his beloved. "You can be sure I will," was the reply.

A few fairly peaceful days passed with Louis keeping his distance from Francine, although his icy stares were still a bit unnerving for her. Over the weekend when Jean left the Aigner residence he noticed, much to his chagrin, Louis was loitering in the area less than a block away. "What are you doing around here Danton," Jean asked sharply. "Why should you care Pontmercy? This is a free country."

"Just stay away from Aigners place, if you know what's good for you."

"I'm on a public street, so don't bother me."

"Make sure you keep off private property or the authorities will be notified."

"You don't scare me," Louis said as they both left the area, headed in different directions.

Several days elapsed before Francine saw her antagonist again. What she heard then left her in a troubled state of mind. Despite trying to ignore him completely, Louis said to her, "I heard Pontmercy saved you in a fire. Maybe the next fire you have, I'll be the one to save you."

After pondering this unsettling information Francine decided to tell Jean what was said, but declined to burden her parents with more worries considering what they had endured in the recent past. When Jean was informed he asked, "Did it appear that Louis had been drinking?"

"No, he seemed to be quite sober and resolute. He's becoming completely impossible," Francine replied. "This is my plan of action, dear, listen and see if you agree. Starting tonight I'll be in the area of your home after dark on a reconnaissance mission, so to speak. I'll stay until midnight for a few days, or even a week, and determine if Louis has something malicious in mind."

"Wonderful Jean, we can't really go to the police unless he actually breaks the law in some way."

"I'm not going to enter the house, Francine. We'll discuss this whenever we talk here on campus."

"Agreed. Incidentally Jean, I'm really thankful for your concern and your love and friendship as well."

"Until later, my angel," he replied while holding both her hands warmly and looking intently into those eyes that could melt a glacier.

Four long evenings passed for Jean and he began to think the entire venture was a waste of time. The following night, shortly after midnight, all that changed. A hooded figure was moving toward the Aigner gate. Once in the yard the figure moved stealthily toward the house, carrying a sack with him. Jean quietly closed the distance between himself and the Aigner property. The figure appeared to be pouring a substance around the base of the wooden porch. Now inside the yard, Jean moved closer. The figure was now igniting some papers or rags at the porches base. As flames sprang up Jean hastened to intervene. The surprised figure wheeled around with the sound of oncoming footsteps. Jean pulled the figure away and simultaneously ripped off his hood.

"You!, Louis Danton. You've gone too far."

"And you, Pontmercy, have ruined everything." They began to struggle and Jean threw him roughly to the ground. Louis did not get up. Although Jean had heard a disturbing sound as Louis hit the turf, he rushed over to the porch and beat out the small fire with the sack that Louis had brought.

At that moment Victor and Francine had arrived on the scene. Jean explained the surveillance briefly and imposed on Victor to arrange transportation to the hospital for the unconscious intruder. Louis had apparently hit his head on a large rock when he fell. The fire was extinguished before any damage occurred and they decided to keep the incident between them and not wake up the rest of the household.

The following day the authorities were notified about the attempted arson and the injury sustained by Danton. The police later confirmed that Louis had sustained a concussion and a dislocated shoulder. Jean and Francine, along with Victor, conferred about the situation and decided to wait until Louis recovered and left the hospital to press criminal charges. It was possible Louis had learned his lesson and with a minimal amount of damage, it might be well to save the family from adverse publicity.

On the day following Louis' release from the hospital, a letter was delivered by courier to Jean. He was completely shocked to find he was summoned for a court appearance in a few days. The charge was assault and battery and the complainant was Louis Danton.

This is an appropriate time to bring the reader up to date concerning a recent retirement party held in the finest hall in the city of Paris. The retiring individual was none other than Rene Duquette, the foremost prosecuting attorney in the city. He was bowing out amid much fanfare and celebration. The only negative incident in his entire career was a defeat in court to Marius Pontmercy, back in the thirties. Rene remained bitter about that decision and hoped for years to face him again in courtroom battle. That day never came. Hope as he may, their paths did not cross again. However, M. Duquette did have hope left in his compelling quest. He had a son, just now entering the arena as new prosecuting attorney. Dante Duquette, every bit a self-centered viper like his father. And the total disdain for the Pontmercy name was indeed passed down to the next generation.

Marius looked up from the stack of papers on his desk and was surprised to see his son entering the office. "Jean, what brings you here today?"

"I don't need money, if that's what you're thinking father," he replied, trying to sound cheerful.

"Actually I'm here on a more serious matter. I believe your professional services will be required in a short time." Jean proceeded to relate the whole story to his father.

"Of course I'll be there as your defense counsel. I'm surprised that rascal Danton thinks he can make those charges stick."

"I don't trust him one bit, Father. He must have some sort of trick or charade planned."

"Well Jean, I assume we'll find out next week."

The Aigner residence was the scene of a major family conference over the weekend. The parents now aware of the happenings of the past couple of weeks, were not too happy about being kept in the dark concerning Francine's problems as she was being stalked. They were, however, noticing a closer bonding between their daughter and Jean and were beginning to realize that in the near future they would be losing a daughter and gaining a son-in-law.

Victor now respected Jean more than when they first met and added his input by saying, "Jean, you can count on me to be there at the hearing. I'm sure your father would want me as well as Francine to attend."

"That's nice of you brother. I'm happy to see you're staying involved, without any coaxing," Francine said.

"I'm proud of you too, Victor," added fifteen year old Lucile. As the discussion was winding down, Jean ended with a more somber note. "By the way, Louis will be represented by a new prosecutor, Dante Duquette. My father won his first case against his father years ago and it seems their family never forgot the case and became embittered over the years. Next week will probably be very interesting."

THE HEARING

A mid-week hearing in the judges chambers had been scheduled to inquire into the possibilities of pressing criminal charges. The Aigners' charges of harassment and vandalism were on hold pending the outcome of the 'Danton' complaint which had been filed earlier. Judge Laforge was hearing the case without the presence of a jury.

Jean arrived with Francine and Victor and they joined Marius who was already present and checking his notes on the case.

The counsel for the defense greeted the trio, "Is there anything else I need to know? After a negative response he continued, "Have you seen Danton yet? I'm expecting only him and Duquette. Let me know if there are any others in their group."

When the prosecutor and his client made their way into the chambers, another young man was with them. Jean and Francine both recognized him vaguely as being a student who occasionally was seen with Louis around the university. This information was passed on to Marius, with Francine adding, "I think his name is Nolet."

Dante Duquette began his well rehearsed story to the judge. "My client was walking in the area of the Aigner residence and noticed a small fire under their porch. When he rushed to put it out, he was attacked by the defendant Jean Pontmercy." Dante pointed in his direction and then continued, "As a result of the assault my client sustained a concussion and a dislocated shoulder. He is seeking costs of medical treatment at the hospital and all fees incurred by this hearing."

The next one to speak was Marius. "There is no truth to any of that rhetoric. My client, who is seeing the Aigners' daughter socially, caught Louis Danton deliberately setting fire to the porch and stopped him. The extent of the injury was accidental due to his head striking a rock. Let it also be known that my client was in the area because he was watching the Aigner residence due to stalking and harassment of Francine by Louis Danton. We request these charges be dismissed in order for us to pursue vandalism charges against Danton."

Duquette then questioned Victor and Francine, who were under oath. "Did either of you witness the attack on my client?" Both answered no, as they came out of the house moments after the incident took place.

The only question Marius had for Francine was, "Is it true Louis was bothering you around the university?" "Yes, he certainly was," came the reply. After she returned to her seat, Duquette called another to the stand.

"Fernand Nolet, please come forward. Is it true as I described in my opening remarks, how the defendant attacked my client?"

Yes, we were walking together in the street. When the commotion began, I fled rather than get involved at the time.

However, I was there long enough to concur with your opening statement."

"Thank you M. Nolet. No further questions," Duquette concluded.

Marius saw the opening he was looking for to exploit the inexperience of the prosecutor and the obvious lie told by the current witness. He needed something to offset the effect of the heavily bandaged Danton, which may extract some sympathy from Judge LaForge.

"Fernand, have you ever been in court before?" Marius began. "No, I have not."

"And you realize you're under oath?"

"Yes, that's correct."

"Do you know the penalty for perjury, even for a hearing like this?"

"No, I didn't think this was the same as a trial," the witness answered as he began to shift his weight nervously in the seat he occupied.

"Fernand, are you telling the truth in this matter?"

"Objection!" said Duquette in a loud voice.

"Overruled, I want to see where this leads," the judge dictated.

"Fernand, I don't think you want to have a police record at this stage of your young life."

"A prison record? That's not for me. This was all Louis' idea. He paid me 50 francs to appear at this hearing. It was supposed to be easy money, but it didn't turn out that way."

At this point in the proceedings an argument erupted between Louis and Fernand, with Duquette becoming upset and quite annoyed with the behavior and the reliability of the witness. Judge LaForge called sternly for order before the situation got out of hand. He then dismissed the charges with strict warnings to both the witness and to Louis about their conduct and the conspiracy they had obviously plotted.

As for Dante Duquette, he should have bided his time and waited for a more favorable opportunity to oppose Marius in court. In his eagerness to avenge his father's sole defeat in court, he moved too hastily and his inexperience was apparent.

THE AFTERMATH

When the dust had settled, the Aigners chose not to press charges and thus hoped to avoid unwanted, adverse publicity. Louis wrote a letter of apology and agreed to transfer to another university in a different city. Oh, he agreed on the surface, in order to diffuse the current situation but he did not intend to leave the area on a note of complete humiliation.

Louis kept an extremely low profile in another part of the city, while enlisting a new pair of eyes and ears in the university to keep tabs on the now despised pair. He fully intended to enjoy the last laugh in this drama before it reached its ultimate completion.

After slightly more than three weeks since the hearing had transpired, the break he had hoped for, arrived. Andre, the student contact arrived with some interesting information for Louis.

"I heard something this morning, Louis, that should lift you from the doldrums." "Wonderful! Tell me quickly, friend." "Quite by accident I heard the two lovebirds talking about their weekend plans. I was on some steps, leaning against a stone wall when I heard voices on the other side. At first I thought it was only idle chatter, of which I had no interest. I continued to study my notes, for I had an exam coming up."

"Get to the point, Andre. I've been waiting for weeks." "Of course, Louis. They kept talking — naturally I couldn't see them but when he said her name, 'Francine', my attention peaked considerably. This very weekend, Saturday night if you will, they'll be at the quarry outside the city. Beautiful view, full moon, very romantic for a couple in love." "Don't make me sick, Andre. Jean Pontmercy will never be in my class as a lover." "Now who can be the judge of that, Louis?" "Any number of lovely ladies in Paris, that's who, my friend." "If you say so. Well, you have the information I was paid to obtain and now I'll be on my way. Don't do anything that will land you in prison." "Save your concerns for your exams, Andre, and let me devise something unpleasant for the two lovers."

Speaking of the adoring pair, they were much relieved to believe Louis was out of their lives forever. And they were indeed just as Andre had overheard, intending to have dinner Saturday evening and then proceed with a leisurely walk to the hills outside the city, just above the quarry. In fact, the previous evening Francine said to Jean, "The weather has been quite nice, dearest, let's take a long walk up to the hills. I'd love to see Paris at dusk from such a gorgeous vantage point." "A similar thought had crossed my mind as well, but I wasn't quite sure what your reaction would be. The area right above the quarry is the highest elevation in the vicinity and should afford a marvelous view."

"Then it's agreed, Jean. We'll dress for a more casual dinner than usual and then make our way toward higher elevations." "Well put, my love. But keep one thing in mind. When I'm with you, the view is always most excellent and I'm transported to elevations higher than the Matterhorn."

"I'm flattered indeed, Jean, that you feel like that. As for me, I can only say I have a great feeling of love and warmth and security when I'm with you. Much like that of early childhood with both parents near and in the envelopment of a loving home atmosphere."

"I'll be seeing you soon, darling, Saturday afternoon for our supper and stroll in the hills." "Until then," said she, as she became the recipient of a tender good bye hug and kiss on the cheek.

Friday evening near dusk, Louis decided to walk the trails leading to the quarry area, much the same way as a general in the army would reconnoiter the countryside before a large battle. He muttered to himself, this will teach them a lesson not to match wits with a Danton. And certainly not to humiliate him in public or steal his lady friend. They both will pay, I'm just not sure how high the price will be.

Louis smiled sarcastically with the knowledge that the area was fairly deserted. He passed six or eight well scattered people, some in pairs, at the lower elevations and only two men in the vicinity of the quarry. One appeared to be a student, perhaps on an assignment, and one nondescript older individual who seemed to be walking aimlessly' looking frequently up at the trees, such as a birdwatcher might do.

After reaching the upper rim over looking the quarry, Louis studied the grounds more intently. He looked down over the edge of the rim and sure enough, just as he had heard, the drop was straight down to the granite rocks below. Was it 80 feet, or 100 feet, or 120 feet, he couldn't tell for certain, but it was a long way down. A long way down, not to a feather pillow, but to bone-crushing granite on the quarry's floor. Louis walked back 30 or 40 feet to the edge of the trees and turned to gaze out over the peaceful city. The moon was almost full and seemed to hang over the quarry and could easily mesmerize two love-struck creatures the following evening. His foot hit something as he walked away. The object was a tree limb and was immediately picked up. The solid limb was hefted by Louis and found to his liking. He broke off a two-foot piece at the narrow end, leaving him a sturdy five-foot limb, fairly straight, about three or four inches in diameter at the larger end which tapered down to two inches and weighed in the neighborhood of twenty five or thirty pounds. This will do well, Louis said out loud, as he contemplated rushing the couple when they approached the edge of the rim, as they most surely would, and battering the pair over the edge with the stout limb. The five-foot length of the limb would allow Louis some insurance, should there be last second detection of his charge. Yes, Louis had made his decision. The price would be high for causing his shame. They would pay the ultimate price — their lives.

Jean arrived at the Aigner's shortly before five o'clock and both he and Francine were dressed casually for a light supper and their extended walk. "How about L'Heureux's place this evening?" he inquired of her. "Of course, that's fine, dearest," Francine answered. After a pleasant meal and some browsing in the city, the couple made their way toward the hills outside of town. It was around seven o'clock when Jean made the following statement as they approached the trails, "We must begin our descent by eight o'clock so we'll have enough light remaining to see our way clearly enough. " "Agreed. That should allow ample time to spend on the bluff and enjoy the awesome spectacle of a full moon and Paris aglow for another splendid evening."

Finally they passed the fringe of trees and proceeded toward the edge of the rim overlooking first the quarry and then the city. "Breathtaking to say the least, my love," Jean sighed. "I wouldn't want to be here with anyone else," Francine whispered softly.

Jean smiled and looked into her sparkling, yet inquisitive eyes, noticed a small tear of happiness trickling down her cheek and was about to speak when the stillness was shattered by a twig snapping a short distance behind them.

Louis had been waiting in the trees for the detested couple to make their appearance and he wasn't disappointed. He had seen no one this evening since the half way point ascending the trail. His hiding place proved to be a scant fifty yards from the vantage point the couple had selected along the rim to view the city.

Quietly, Louis melted among the trees to obtain a direct line from which to make his charge. Finally the right moment came. He balanced the limb carefully in his hands and moved slowly forward, slightly crouched. Upon reaching twenty feet from the couple, Louis charged! Blinded with anger his third or fourth step came down firmly on a large twig and it snapped.

Jean, alerted by some sixth sense, turned instantly and saw a form bearing down on them. In one liquid motion he turned and thrust Francine and himself to the ground at the edge of the rim. An instant later, Louis' charge carried him to the edge as well. Failing to hit something solid had carried Louis' charge too far! He teetered at the brink. The limb dropped over the edge, followed by the bearer of that limb. Aaugh! A sickening thud far below, and then silence.

Francine was sobbing, but she was safe. For the second time her life was saved by the one she now loved dearly. Both were scraped and bruised and a little dusty, but otherwise they were fine. "Who could have done this?" Jean said, more resembling a statement than a question. "That couldn't be Louis down there, could it? We haven't seen him since the hearing," Francine continued. Arm in arm, the pair started down the trail. Taking the path nearest the quarry bed, Jean walked over to the body as Francine kept her distance from the point of impact. The body was turned over and in the moonlight Jean saw that it was indeed Louis Danton.

The unfortunate incident was reported to the proper authorities and the couple was finally able to continue on with their lives in a more normal manner. A private funeral was held for the victim. There were very few attendees.

THE WEDDING

The following spring, when their last days at the university were winding down, Jean and Francine were planning a late June wedding. Or, shall we say the Aigner's were actually doing the vast majority of the planning. Mme. Aigner, a doting mother to say the least, was now in all her glory in the preparation of this huge event. The first of her two daughters, to be united in marriage was undoubtedly destined to be one of the two or three major highlights in the life of this charming woman, well known in the society world of Paris.

Content to stay clear of all these necessary preliminaries, Jean was happy to know just the date and the time, now that Francine was committed to him. That commitment alone brought enough wonder and joy to last two life times. The winning of Francine's hand was indeed paramount to Jean, dwarfing his longing to be a lawyer and even blurring his devotion to the rest of his family.

A potential problem, albeit a minor one, arose when Francine asked him, "Jean, I'm planning to have six bridesmaids. Will you have any trouble matching that number among your closer friends?" "Oh, I think I'll manage, darling. I hope your family won't become paupers before this is over." "Not likely, although they will probably be parting with about 50,000 francs, considering the hall and food for 300 guests. And, of course, my gown and other apparel and our honeymoon trip." "Sounds wonderful to me." "It will be," Francine continued "and since you had no preference for our honeymoon destination, we shall be traveling to London and then seeing as much of the British Isles as we can in three weeks." "I couldn't have made a better choice, darling." "I've always wanted to visit England and now we both have the perfect opportunity." "I'm a very fortunate man, and as long as we are together, even a small town would seem like London to me."

As the wedding drew nearer, Jean decided to ask Victor to be his best man. The two had progressed from just tolerating each other to a high level of respect and warm regard. Of course it was

Victor who had the larger change in attitude, as Jean was, from the beginning, eager to become close to all of the Aigners, for Francine's sake. The wedding party was large and perhaps three-fourths of the total number of guests would be invited by the bride and her family.

Before long, the big day arrived. The last Saturday in June, 1857, began cloudy and overcast but was destined to turn out with mostly blue skies and a pleasant breeze. The large church was filled well before the eleven AM nuptials were scheduled. The immense stained glass windows on the east side of the structure glowed with warm sunlight. The wedding party fanned out across the front of the church and seemed as beautiful as the abundance of flowers so gorgeously arranged throughout the majestic edifice.

M. Aigner escorted Francine down the aisle toward her destiny as the onlookers were amazed that the ravishing one was even more dazzling in her wedding gown. Jean looked striking, the image of his father on his wedding day, twenty four years prior.

After the ceremony and the vows were exchanged, the wedding party and all the guests made their way to the grandest and nearly the largest hall in the city. So many well-wishers visited their table, the newlyweds could scarcely finish their meal. Fortunate for them, food was not uppermost on their minds. They were dreamily consumed with each other, with other considerations secondary. By this time they were eager for the departure of their late afternoon coach, taking them on the first leg of their honeymoon trip to England.

Shortly after their arrival in London the following afternoon, Jean asked his new bride, "What have you scheduled for us today, dearest? I'm sure you have quite an agenda ready." "You know the answer to that question, darling. We have much to see and do, I'm sure you'll enjoy yourself." "There's no doubt in my mind that I will," he replied.

And, as they were blessed with fine weather, other than a few season showers, they most certainly did have a wonderful time. The happy couple boated on the Thames, visited the tower of London and many other historic sites. They managed to squeeze in a three-day side trip to Ireland as well.

Before leaving the London area, Francine read about a new structure in the planning stages for the city. "Listen to this, Jean. There will be a huge clock tower built at the eastern end of the houses of Parliament, Westminster. It will have a 13 ton bell. Isn't that awesome, dear?" "It probably is the largest of its kind on the face of the earth. Some day, hopefully, Paris will construct a monument that will be known worldwide," Jean replied.

When the newlyweds returned home it could be said that they were even more in love than before they departed, if that were possible. They settled in a modest apartment near the business section of the city. Despite an offer from her father, Francine refused to draw on her future inheritance, preferring to utilize only their own income. In less than three years they moved to a fair sized home with a half acre of property. The main reason for the move? The first of three children born between 1860 and 1866, had arrived.

But avoid foolish questions, and contentions and strivings about the law; for they are unprofitable and vain.

Titus 3:9

Chapter VI

PIERRE

. . . .

EPONINE - AUTUMN 1853

Shortly before Eponine Pontmercy celebrated her sixteenth birthday she attended a church social which was held for young people in their mid to upper teens and even some single people in their very early twenties. A warm sunny afternoon in early fall promised to be a memorable Sunday for the 25 or 30 attendees who were present. Twenty one year old Guy Fredette, who had just recently been ushered out of the depths of an introverted existence and experienced a profound coming-of-age encounter with a flamboyant, recently widowed woman in her early thirties, was there as well. He was there because he knew Eponine would attend. The young girl he had noticed and then admired secretly for the last year and a half during mass now looked different to him since his shackles of ignorance were broken. The long blonde hair that he often longed to run his fingers through was even longer and blonder, if that were possible. The sweet face and sparkling eyes were rapidly gaining maturity. But now Guy was familiar with what awaited him under the layers of petticoats worn by the one who fascinated him so. Even when he learned she was about a year younger than originally surmised his judgement was clouded by the fragrances she used and the way she dressed and moved about so gracefully. Guy, at present, considered himself an experienced lover and he was determined to explore all the possibilities with someone fresh and new, especially now that the older woman had made it plain she was no longer mused by his naivete.

"Good afternoon, Mlle. Pontmercy," Guy said pleasantly at his first opportunity to introduce himself. "Nice to meet you. Please call me Eponine," she returned and asked his name as she truly had no idea who he was. After identifying himself, Guy continued, "I first saw you taking communion and became quite captivated over the last few months. I really enjoy the church and religious things," he stretched the truth greatly with the hope of impressing his young acquaintance. "The church and your beliefs should be a main part of your life, Guy. " "I agree. Perhaps you'd like to walk outside in the gardens, as some of the others are doing, Eponine?" "Why, I suppose so. There are some lovely flowers in those gardens." Guy's main objective was to see how quickly she could be extracted from the main body of persons at the social.

There were beautiful and aromatic flowers to be sure, but Guy found no opening to get closer to Eponine as she was constantly chatting with other guests and moving about freely. He reasoned to himself that he should not act too hastily anyway and ruin possibilities for future exploitation of this budding princess.

As the afternoon was winding down, Guy did muster his courage to ask the following, "Permission to walk you to your home after mass next Sunday, Eponine?" "I think that would be alright, so long as my parents agree. And I think they probably will—See you next Sunday."

Guy gloated to himself as the social began to disband. This was another step in the right direction, he figured. The week most certainly would drag by slowly but the wait would be worthwhile.

The following Sunday the pair began walking to the Pontmercy home, without any formal introductions being exchanged between Guy and the parents. The fifteen minute stroll ended at the house and Guy wondered if he would be invited inside. That was not to be the case and he decided to become more talkative at that point. "Very nice place you have here Eponine. I suppose you have your own room?" "Yes, I do. See that window on the second floor?" she answered, pointing to a window located about mid-way down the side of the house. "Sure, I see it," Guy replied. He also saw a large tree whose trunk was about twenty feet from the side of the house, but had branches that extended much closer. Already his mind was working toward a plan where that tree could be utilized in the near future. "I must go in now, Guy. We'll probably see each other again next Sunday." The words held no real promise but they were enough to bring him back from his thoughts relative to the tree. "Bye, Eponine. See you next week."

Guy was chuckling to himself as he walked home, maybe I'll see you before you see me. He would be paying careful attention to the weather in the coming days, ideally looking for a rain-free moonless dark night. During his youth, Guy loved to climb trees and was now hoping to recall some of those skills in order to make himself a spectator about 15 feet outside Eponine's bedroom window.

Although Monday and Tuesday proved to be rainy days, Guy bundled himself up to stay dry and made his way to observe the Pontmercy residence from a distance. Both nights the desired room on the second floor was darkened between 9:15 and 9:30. At this time of the year, it became fairly dark by 8:00 PM so Guy decided to ascend the tree at approximately 8:30 and obtain a bird's-eye view, so to speak. He noticed, also, that there were no close houses on the tree side of the home either.

Wednesday arrived dry but overcast, and Guy made his way toward 'her' house in the deepening dusk. Few people were on the streets and he quietly made his way into the yard and over to the tree. While climbing slowly he heard faintly from within the house, the father saying to the daughter, "Good night angel." Well, right on schedule, Guy said to himself, that was good news at about 8:40 PM.

A few minutes later a lamp came on and the room was bathed in a soft light. Guy edged further out on the stout limb that was positioned in a direct line toward the right side of the window frame. Eponine walked over to her vanity and sat down. What was that she was carrying, a book? No, maybe it was a diary as she appeared to be writing something on its pages. After a short time a hair brush was produced and she began stroking the golden, shoulder-length locks. Quite a vantage point Guy mused to himself. He calculated he was about twelve feet from the window and she was around eight to ten feet from the window on the inside. How long would this hair procedure last? She must be counting the strokes and the total was high. Oh oh, here she comes toward the window. I must be completely still and quiet, he told himself. Alright, just a breath of fresh air and a quick glance out toward the street. Now where did she go? The sound of a closet door closing and there she was again. Guy noticed she carried an article of clothing. What's this, tomorrow's outfit? No, there's not enough bulk to it. Must be the sleeping apparel, he thought as his pulse rate began to quicken. From his location he could see the vanity, the chair and half of her bed which was near the window. The window itself was curtained on the inside, but apparently the curtains were tied back at the middle.

The outer garments were removed and placed carefully on the chair. Guy now sensed he had underestimated the extent of the physical development of this young princess. He now observed some sort of toe-touching exercise that was probably part of her evening ritual. With those maneuvers completed it finally appeared that the remaining under garments of the upper torso were about to be removed. He had already observed the legs to mid-thigh and now his palms that gripped the limb were becoming sweaty. The garment was loosened around the waist, her arms crossed in front of her as if to lift off all that remained when a door slammed down below.

The slamming door stopped Eponine momentarily and as she was about to resume, the barking of a dog again stopped the procedure. Much to Guy's chagrin, the barking sound came from directly under the tree he was encamped in. He cursed softly to himself, a stupid dog. That's one thing I didn't count on. I should have checked to see if they owned any animals.

Marius had obtained the dog the previous fall as he now engaged in a bit of hunting from time to time to create a change of pace from his demanding profession. The dog usually had his final run outdoors a bit later but as he seemed restless this evening his master decided to let him take an early run as well.

By the time Guy made his way down the tree, Marius, Marcel and Eponine were all out there and saw who he was. Marius told him, "Get out of here, never come back or speak to my daughter again or you'll surely be arrested." Guy scurried out of the yard, hoping the dog would not be turned loose. Eponine, quite shocked by his behavior, vowed it would be a long time before she trusted anyone of the opposite sex again.

CITIZENS ARREST

Pierre Lacroix worked very hard in the years that followed the disastrous shooting accident at the barricades in 1848. As time went by he seemed to sense that his opportunities for employment would be greatly limited. In reality he probably wasn't cut out for heavy manual labor or farming anyway. So he concentrated on finance, taking all the courses he could in mathematics, accounting and bookkeeping. By applying himself in a specialized field, and having limited extra-curricular activities due to his handicap, he excelled. Graduating in the top ten percent of his university class, he had very little difficulty obtaining a position in an investment firm. For the sake of continuity, nine years had passed since the incident at the barricade.

During his first year with the investment firm, Pierre was required to make daily trips to the bank for the purpose of depositing securities and cash. He was there every afternoon and sometimes made a late morning trip when the volume of business was heavy. The bank which the firm utilized, Paris National, was barely a five minute walk and he enjoyed the fresh air and the brief respite from the daily routine. However, he enjoyed something much more in recent weeks. Something that could have easily replaced food and drink for this young man. As the reader may have already suspected, that 'something' was really a 'someone', in the form of a gorgeous, blue-eyed blonde.

This particular individual also made deposits for her clothing store employer and was seen by Pierre about three times a week, when he was fortunate. Through his camaraderie with one of the bank employees, Pierre soon learned she was Mlle. Pontmercy, recently employed by the Aigner clothing establishment. She usually arrived between 3 PM and 4 PM and her new admirer found ways of stalling and somehow prolonging his banking stop in the hopes their paths may cross.

Something should be noted at this time relative to Pierre's handicap, which did not really handicap him all that much. Certainly there were things he could never do, but there were many more things he could do and do well. With his right leg amputated half way between the hip and the knee, Pierre had developed three options for his daily walk through life. From the time he reached his full adult height, about seventeen, he had acquired a wooden leg. He also utilized a crutch or a cane, depending on his mood on a given day. The wooden prosthesis was fine but at times he preferred the cane or crutch to the limp which accompanied the use of the artificial limb.

One warm late-spring afternoon Pierre felt he was experiencing a taste of heaven. Entering the bank just after him, and standing only a few feet away at the next teller was that golden-haired object of his affection Mlle. Pontmercy. No words had ever passed between them, but Pierre turned and somewhat awkwardly uttered, "Good afternoon." The lovely head turned in his direction, smiled politely and nodded a bit. His transaction of business drawn out to the utmost, Pierre walked over to the counter near the door and fastidiously adjusted his receipts. What was taking her so long he wondered as he wished to see the angel leave the bank before he did.

Just then Pierre noticed a commotion between a teller and a patron further down the floor. The patron, a rather shabbily dressed man probably in his mid-twenties, suddenly bolted toward the door carrying a large envelope. "Stop him!" shouted the teller, "Stop thief." The eight or ten other patrons who had an outside chance to do any stopping were in various stages of complete surprise or shock.

Pierre, however, was alert and watching for a heavenly body, saw a meteor running for the door with stolen money. Pierre, using his crutch this day, turned it into a weapon. Whirling quickly around, he swung the crutch in a arc that knocked the feet out from under the fleeing robber and he fell heavily to the floor. "Not so fast, fellow. You're not going anywhere," Pierre announced in a loud voice. He was immediately over the stunned man and reversing his crutch, pinned him firmly to the floor, his neck encircled by the upper end of the crutch. Since his accident Pierre developed above average upper body strength. The would-be robber flailed about for some minutes in a futile attempt to free himself. It did not take long for the authorities to arrive and take the man into custody.

As he was catching his breath and regaining his composure, Pierre heard a voice from behind him say, "That was a very brave act on your part, Monsieur." He turned, saw that it was 'she' who had spoken, and he tingled down to his remaining five toes. Not really knowing if she wanted to know his name, he stammered, "Monsieur Lacroix, that is — Pierre Lacroix, or just call me Pierre. Surprising himself he added, "And you are?" "I'm Eponine Pontmercy. I believe I've seen you here before, haven't I?"

"I come here often," he answered, trying to hide his surprise that she had noticed him.

"Well it's not every day something like this happens Pierre," she continued. "But, now I must return to the store. Perhaps we'll meet again."

Pierre, sensing this may be his one big opportunity, asked "Is it possible we could get together for lunch? If you're not seeing someone else, of course."

"I think I'd like that. Let's say early next week, and no, I'm not seeing anyone else right now."

"I'll be sure to see you on Friday and we can finalize the date and time," Pierre added.

As they parted and he hurried back to work, Pierre wondered what she meant by the words 'right now'. Was she just between suitors? She could certainly have her pick, if she so chose. The truth was, Eponine chose to pick no one because of that unpleasant experience with Guy Fredette shortly before she turned sixteen years of age. Since then she decided to concentrate on her career and put romance on the back burner. Alas, Pierre didn't know this and when confronted with such beauty could only surmise the direct opposite.

MUTUAL ADMIRATION

The life of Eponine Pontmercy, now twenty years of age, was unfolding very much the opposite of her namesake. For the former Eponine T., who died at the barricade long before her twentieth birthday, life was on a downhill spiral by the time she reached the age of ten. With the demise of the family business, her environment decayed with crime and corruption with each passing year.

When Eponine P. reached the age of thirteen, or perhaps it was fourteen, she inquired why she was named what she was, considering the fact that she knew of no relatives living or dead, so named. She was informed of the whole story, with nothing held back, and was amazed at the love shown by such an unlikely person.

As for Mlle. Pontmercy herself, she favored her mother almost as much as Jean resembled his father. Golden hair, sparkling blue eyes, just a shade taller and with all the grace and poise as a deer bounding through a meadow. She had a strong sense of caring for the mentally and physically disabled, especially children. She spent part of two summers caring for these children at the same hospital where her mother spent so many volunteer hours.

And now there was the recent encounter at the bank with Pierre Lacroix. The young man had a disability and he also had courage. He certainly would never need her help for anything in life's daily routine. She did not look on him as anything less than a complete man and although she had just met him, she was drawn to him with feelings she could not explain. She would go to lunch with him and get to know him better.

After Pierre confirmed the luncheon date for the following Tuesday, he realized it must be cleared with his supervisor. He had some second thoughts and wondered why he hadn't asked for a dinner meeting after the work day was complete. He approached M. Gilbert somewhat nervously with his request. "Why, of course," was the reply. "Take all the time you need. You've been a model employee since the day you began, and you know Pierre, I was young once too." Pierre was supremely grateful with this fatherly approval and could only say, "Thank you, thank you," accompanied by a 'bon voyage' sized handshake.

Tuesday finally arrived for Pierre. He could hardly believe he would be spending a full hour with someone he considered as enchanting as an angel from a distant planet. If someone told him that his luncheon guest was anticipating their meeting with almost as much enthusiasm, but for different reasons, he would have been amazed. Different reasons in that he was reaching for a heavenly body while she was more interested in down to earth realism, honesty and sincerity. As providence would have it, neither of these two very different persons needed to look any further.

"Good day Mlle. Pontmercy," were the first words Eponine heard as she exited the building of her employment. "And good day to you Pierre, and I think we can be on a 'first name' basis for our lunch today." "I'm glad you said that, the informality is much more relaxing," Pierre replied, having been a bit nervous up to that point.

The restaurant was located about half way between their work places. Although Pierre lived frugally, he chose one of the better eating places, for price was virtually no object for this meal. The conversation flowed easily between the two. A little about their occupations, but a lot more relative to family life and their education and expectations in life.

After dessert, Pierre said, "As much as I'm enjoying myself, I must be prompt in returning to the office. We may want to do this again in the near future. "I'd enjoy that Pierre. I've had a wonderful time."

As they left the restaurant, Pierre's attentions were pried away momentarily to a man lounging against a nearby lamp post. The man was staring at the couple and scowling angrily in their direction. When Pierre noticed him, he looked at Pierre and then down at the periodical he was carrying. Pierre thought the man looked somewhat familiar but he wasn't sure. His thoughts quickly returned to the one he was escorting.

THE GAUTHIER BROTHERS

Yvon and Yves Gauthier were born a year apart but in many ways were as alike as if they were twins. The elder, Yvon, was a little taller and heavier with a more sinister countenance. Both had dark hair, bushy eyebrows, and a swarthy complexion. They shared a fierce loyalty for each other and both were hellraisers and thieves.

The previous week Yvon had been waiting outside the bank to run interference for Yves after he burst outside with the loot. This was to be their second bank robbery in a little less than a month.

They planned to leave the area completely and would have plenty of money available for them to spend a year or two in parts of Italy and Spain, cultivating some new underworld connections. All those plans were thwarted by a cripple and his crutch. To say that Yvon was furious would be a gross understatement.

During his brief ten minute visit with his incarcerated brother, Yvon vowed to damage the cripple's other leg. He would need two crutches for the rest of his life and if his prissy girl friend got in the way, she would meet the same fate. Yves could only answer, "Whatever you do, big brother, don't get caught, and don't leave the country without me. I think my chance will come to break out of this place before my trial."

"Don't worry about me, Yves. Just find a way to get out of there. Brothers like us shouldn't be separated for ten years or more."

"Right. I'll get word to you if I need outside help for my break. See you later."

Eponine had not seemed herself around the house recently which prompted the following question from Marius, "You appear to be a bit pre-occupied, Ponine. Is everything going well at work?"

"Oh, sure father," began the reply, "Everything is fine and I really like my job."

"Have you been feeling well lately, I've noticed a change too?" Cosette had joined the conversation. "Of course, Mother, I feel wonderful. As a matter of fact, I met someone recently who I care a great deal for. His name is Pierre."

"That probably explains everything. It has been quite a while since you've cared for a young man. He must be very special to capture your complete attention," Marius added.

"He's the one I told you about. You know, the attempted bank holdup. We had lunch together and I'd really like to see him again."

"You go right ahead Ponine. He seems like a very caring and courageous individual. All men aren't like that opportunistic tyrant that jilted you a couple of years ago," Cosette said with that typically reassuring motherly manner.

"I really appreciate your support on this. I must have the best parents in the city of Paris and I love you both."

At the end of the following week, Pierre awoke in a very good mood. It was Friday, the end of the work week and he was having dinner with the person he cared for most in this universe. Yes it was dinner this time and not lunch. There would be no need to hurry back to work. And tonight there would also be a long and leisurely walk back to Eponine's house.

As Pierre was dressing for work, he thought he heard something on the stairway. He rented a second floor apartment from an elderly couple and it was usually very quiet at this time of the morning. He ducked his head out of the door and glanced down the steps to his private entrance. He saw nothing but it appeared the first floor door had just closed by the clicking sound that he heard. The upper door was kept locked, but never the lower one. He surmised it may have been a neighborhood child.

After the work day was completed and he was seated across the table from his dinner companion at their favorite restaurant, Eponine remarked in general conversation, "A funny thing happened last night at home. We heard a noise outside in the yard and when we looked toward the windows a shadow moved by, illuminated by a street lamp or possibly the moon. Father went outside and looked around for a few minutes, but with no results." "I had a similar experience," Pierre said, and then told of his morning incident. "We'll keep each other informed if anything is stolen."

The dinner date was delightful in every way for both of them. They walked for nearly an hour, taking a long detour on the way to Eponine's house. The pair found they had much in common socially, politically, and also with their long range goals in life. Once, in a more deserted area, they thought someone may have been lurking behind a long row of hedges. When other pedestrians appeared on the block the rustling behind the hedges ceased.

As the happy couple said their 'goodnights' at the Pontmercy gate, Eponine remarked, "I think the time has come for you to meet my parents, Pierre. I'm sure they'd like to have you here for dinner and get to know you."

"That sounds fine with me. Just let me know and I'll be here, you can count on that." "One more thing Pierre, my parents and a few close friends and relatives call me Ponine. It's less formal and I'd really like it if you called me that too."

"I'd love to, actually, anything that makes you happy pleases me as well," Pierre added as he left. "See you during the week, Ponine my dear."

Shortly after Pierre left, a figure emerged from behind a large bush across the street. He checked the area closely and walked by the Pontmercy residence. The address plaque on the gate was read and duly noted. The shadowy figure then dissolved into the night.

REVENGE

The door swung open to the visiting area of the city prison and Yves Gauthier entered the room and sat across from his brother. Yvon spoke first. "How is it behind those walls, brother?" "Not good. I'm making my move tomorrow, after the recreation time. There's a spot I can hide and when the yard is clear, I'm going over the wall using a rope I'll have."

"Be careful little brother," Yvon warned. "I'll be waiting for you, south of the prison."

"When I'm free we'll plan our next heist. We should hit a store this time and skip the banks."

"We'll talk about that later when you get out. We should go out and get drunk first and celebrate your return to the outside world."

"Just be ready for me, Yvon. Shh, they're coming to take me back now."

The following afternoon Yvon was pacing nervously by some trees about fifty yards south of the prison. He looked at his stolen timepiece and mumbled half to himself and half out loud, 'It's getting late, he should have been out by now.' He was beginning to wonder if Yves had planned his break too quickly.

Just then the silence was shattered by a blaring siren. Yvon left the cover of the trees and trained his vision on the south wall. Sure enough, a rope dangled over the wall and almost reached the ground. An arm was thrust over the wall. The siren paused and several shots rang out and then the arm vanished. A sickening chill enveloped Yvon's entire being. He sensed the worst had happened and his brother had been wounded or even killed.

On the other side of the wall events had transpired rather quickly. An inquisitive guard, in checking the count of prisoners returning from the yard, noticed the total to be one short. He immediately sounded the alarm which brought a number of armed guards into the area. A prisoner was spotted attempting to scale the wall and a warning given, "Stop, or you will be shot!" No response. A warning shot was fired and still the man kept climbing. A volley of shots rang out. One shot grazed the prisoner's leg but would not have stopped him, had not another crashed through his neck at the base of the skull. In a strictly pathological sense, the inmate was dead before he hit the ground. So near and yet so far.

The news which he dreaded to hear reached Yvon the following morning. His younger brother was really dead. If he had been furious earlier about this entire scenario, he was now completely livid. He cursed and made vows of revenge. Out loud he raved, "That cripple caused all this. He will pay and pay dearly. Inflicting pain and breaking his other leg will no longer be enough. Not nearly enough. He will pay with his life. I'll get them both. His prissy girlfriend will pay too, just for knowing him. And I'll enjoy every minute of it."

Pierre and Eponine had not exactly fallen in love but rather drifted into love over the past few weeks. Both lived for their now extended banking meetings. Pierre composed some romantic poetry and presented it to Ponine in the bank, not waiting for the next supper engagement. Their everyday routines were performed in a blurred state, waiting patiently for the next time that their eyes would meet. And yes, only recently, when their lips would meet as well. Eponine's inhibitions of the previous few years were finally beginning to slip away. Poor things — they had absolutely no idea what was in store for them in the very near future.

On their next meeting at the bank Eponine said to Pierre, "It looks like this weekend is out for your dinner visit at my place. Father is travelling to London on business for a few days and mother will be joining him."

"That's perfectly alright, Ponine. A delay of a week or two doesn't matter. We can still have dinner in town on Friday again."

"You're very understanding today, Pierre. Having a good day at work?"

"And why wouldn't I, thinking about you most of the day as I do?"

"Is that right. I hope you're concentrating on your work. I wouldn't want you to be fired, then I'd have to pay for dinner," Ponine chided with a smile that would make an iceberg melt.

"No fear of that my little comedian. I'm well liked at the office, my supervisor told me just recently."

"Touché, we must compare our raises next time that they're due."

"We both must leave, you know. I'll stop for you after work on Friday," Pierre said. He kissed her tenderly on the cheek and was on his way.

Thursday was a rainy day and when Pierre was on his way home from work, he thought that someone was following him. He turned several times in an effort to see somebody but without success. The idea was discarded. Soon the work week had ended and he was again on a higher plateau. He would be with the love of his life and he revelled in the opportunity. The evening was, in many ways, almost a carbon copy of the previous week except they noticed their food less and each other more. Afterwards, their walk extended their time together and was lengthened. This particular evening they intended to be out a little later, possibly owing to the fact that Eponine's parents were out of town.

Yvon Gauthier chuckled grimly to himself, "This couple is very predictable." He had been in the shadows near the restaurant and, sure enough, there they were. He was not far behind when they began their stroll. Safely tucked in his belt was his revolver which he had spent a full hour cleaning and oiling during the afternoon. When the pair, who were almost oblivious to their surroundings, reached the most distant point of their walk, which was also the most desolate part of the city, Yvon decided it was time to make his presence known.

With a few long strides he was right behind them and pressing the revolver against Pierre's spine he announced, "Don't turn around and don't make a sound. That's a gun in your back."

Instantly brought back to reality Pierre said, "Don't scream Ponine, I think he means business.

"That's good advice from your friend. Just keep walkin' where I tell you."

After about ten blocks, which included several turns, they reached Yvon's run-down dwelling place.

"Get inside," he said gruffly as he opened the door. They entered and Yvon, keeping the gun in Pierre's back, pushed Eponine roughly to the floor. As she fell her head grazed the corner of a table and prompted an outcry of pain. "Shut up if you know what's good for you," came the order. Noticing some blood trickling down the side of Eponine's face, Pierre tried to help but was rebuffed.

"Now I'll tell you why you're here," Yvon snarled. "You, cripple, stopped my brother in the bank last month and he was arrested." "He broke the law," Pierre blurted out. "Don't interrupt. After he was arrested, my brother tried to escape and was killed and it's all your fault. Do you understand?"

There was no reply. "And now you must pay for what you did. You will die, cripple and then your friend also. But she will die much slower after I have some fun with her first. On second thought, maybe I'll tie you up and make you watch as she loses her virginity," Yvon raved on.

Eponine recoiled in horror at the thought, drawing her legs up and assuming a fetal position. "Leave her alone, you animal," Pierre said as he mustered up all the courage he could. Yvon was trying to decide which despicable act to perform first and moved closer to Pierre. As Eponine was shaking uncontrollably, Pierre was thinking that either being tied up or shot dead, he would be of no help to himself or his beloved. He must take some sort of action immediately.

When Yvon was about two steps away, Pierre lunged forward and using the cane, which he was carrying this evening, swung it in an upward motion hoping to dislodge the revolver from the thug's grasp. Yvon, having decided to kill Pierre first, pulled the trigger a split second after the cane found its mark. The revolver at that instant was pointed upward and the bullet struck Yvon under the chin and coursed upward in a wavy path, burying itself deep in the cerebral cavity. Yvon slumped to the floor with a sickening groan. Ironically Yvon expired just like his brother as he was dead before he reached the floor, forensically speaking.

THE PONTMERCY'S OF PARIS

Pierre realized the end had come for their antagonist and hurried over to where Eponine lay trembling. "Ponine, my dear Ponine. What have I gotten you into? She was still shaking somewhat and some of her tears intermingled with the trickle of blood from her head wound, leaving a pinkish trail down her cheek. "It's not your fault, my love. Who could know this awful thing was possible." Pierre gently wiped her face and held her closely and tenderly for a while. Despite their ordeal just concluded, she looked more beautiful to him than ever before.

The body of Yvon Gauthier was covered by Pierre with a threadbare blanket taken from the bedroom. They went hastily to the nearest medical facility to obtain treatment for Eponine. Pierre then made his way to the nearest police station to report the incident and give his statement. The authorities were quite understanding and arrangements were made to complete a detailed report within a few days.

LOVE - NOT ONLY FOR EACH OTHER

With that most unpleasant and dangerous ordeal now behind them, the happy couple were almost inseparable and totally devoted to each other. The long overdue dinner visit to the Pontmercy's was consummated and many others followed as Pierre found immediate favor with Marius and Cosette.

A few short months passed and one evening Pierre had an important question for his beloved. "Ponine, I'm not sure how to say this. I'd like to ask your parents for your hand in marriage, but........I want to know if you feel the same way I do. I mean, do you love me half as much as I love you? I hope I'm not making a fool of myself." "Oh my dear Pierre, I was hoping and dreaming you'd bring up the subject of marriage. I know my parents will be very happy and, yes, I do love you at least half as much as you love me, and much more besides."

Their wedding took place the following spring and was on a much smaller scale than the extravaganza which the Aigner's created for Jean and Francine. After the ceremony a modest reception was held at the Pontmercy home and included relatives and close friends and numbered in the thirties.

Pierre continued to excel in the investment business and after two years in an apartment, the couple purchased a large older home which required a great deal of repair and maintenance as it had been empty for a lengthy period of time. Another two years of work took place and finally the house was in splendid condition and contained five bedrooms and a large dining room.

To assume the couple was expecting to have a large number of children would be completely inaccurate. In fact they were not able to have any children. And yet, they had eighteen children! How was this possible, one may ask. True, they had no children of their own, but over the course of their married life they cared for eighteen 'foster' children for various lengths of time. From 1862 until 1887 they had as many as three, but never less than one at a time. They gave hope to the hopeless, boys and girls alike. Some were crippled from birth, while others lost limbs in tragic accidents. Three of the number were sightless and all who entered the 'Lacroix House' found a new reason to go on living and loving life. All who found refuge there, blessed Eponine and Pierre and most returned to visit long after their rehabilitation period was over and they were out in the world on their own.

Soon after the third child was taken in, additional help was needed for Eponine. A brief period of interviewing followed, with a strong emphasis on long hours and love and devotion for the children. A single candidate stood out from all the others. She was a very caring and devoted woman in her thirties, her name was Bernadette, and she remained with the Lacroixs for the duration of their ministry and service to the people of Paris and the surrounding communities.

Over the years, Pierre was known to proclaim the following, whenever and wherever an individual or an audience would listen. "The poor and the infirm, especially children, from Paris, or France as a nation, or the whole world for that matter are everyone's responsibility. We must not live unto ourselves alone, but share the burden of those less fortunate than ourselves. In order to point the history we create in the right direction we should endeavor to eliminate apathy and greed and share the many blessings granted to us by our Creator and turn the tide of poverty, fear and mistrust toward an era of giving and peace and brotherly love."

And whosoever shall give to drink unto one of these little ones a cup of cold water only in the name of a disciple, verily I say unto you, he shall in no wise lose his reward.

Matt. 10:42

Chapter VII

GRANDCHILDREN

• •

<u>A FAMILIAR NAME</u>

If anyone had told Cosette and Marius they would become grandparents while still in their forties they probably would not have believed it. Nevertheless, such was the case. In 1860 Charles was born and named for his maternal grandfather. Daughter Bridgette, arrived in 1863 and finally Suzanne in 1866. The family of their first born was now complete. As for the grandparents, they remained at the place of their honeymoon. They both adored the old Gillenormand home, the place of healing and recovery for Marius and the consummation of their love. The home that watched their children grow and mature was too precious for them to ever consider leaving.

Mlle. Gillenormand had passed away in 1853 at the age of 77. Marcel and Marie left in 1856 for retirement and a small cottage further south. A year later Yvette became the only staff member, mainly for cooking and cleaning as the couple entertained frequently as lawyers generally do. She was good company for Cosette. And the Baron was still the handsome Baron and the Lark had become a Swan.

Bridgette, middle child of Jean and Francine, had a childhood not unlike her siblings. Very normal and unspectacular in every way. Her adult life and the one who eventually became her spouse invites us to explore those events in preemption of the others.

In 1859 a boy was born to a middle class family with strong military ties. As possible names for the child were discussed the boy's father had a choice in mind and could not be dissuaded. Stories had been passed down to him of an uncle whom he had never met. A man of vision who died at a young age. A born leader who had hopes and ideas for a new and different France. A person who had died in his early twenties while leading a group of men behind a barricade. A man admired by his foes and then shot dead in June of 1832. Enjolras!

At the end of 1875, the national assembly at last dissolved itself, and the provisional phase of the third republic came to an end. Rival factions soon developed among the new republican regime. The two main rival factions were known as Opportunist and Radical. One strong supporter of the Radical left was a young man whose namesake was also somewhat radical many years previous. In 1879 this second year university student was talking politics to a newly acquired female admirer. "These Opportunist will be nothing but trouble," said Enjolras, who was unable to look anywhere but into the piercing blue eyes of this new admirer. Although several years younger, Bridgette Pontmercy often walked by the university on her way home from high school. She enjoyed the study of history and just recently politics and the frequent outdoor debates among the college students.

"Why do you say that?" she wanted to know.

"That faction knows only how to postpone decisions and offer compromises, young lady."

"Well, my father's a lawyer, Monsieur. I will ask his opinion on the matter."

"Fine. Let me know where he stands and if we differ, I'll visit him for a small debate."

Without really knowing it, Enjolras had opened the door for a future relationship. Whereas he was only interested talking politics, she was obeying other instincts far stronger than mere politics. While he saw her as a schoolgirl with awesome eyes and lovely dark brown hair much younger than himself, she saw him several years in the future where three or four years worth of age difference would hardly matter.

Two weeks elapsed before Bridgette saw him again and she did not waste the opportunity presented to her.

"M. Enjolras, my father would like to meet you."

The tall student with wavy blonde hair turned and replied, "Oh yes, I remember. Some evening next week, hopefully."

"I'll let you know. Will you be here tomorrow?" she inquired.

"I'll be here unless its' raining. In that case I'll be in the auditorium."

The following week found Enjolras strolling over to Bridgette's house, only a ten minute walk from the university. Dessert and some friendly conversation were on the menu and he was looking forward to an interesting evening. The time was slightly past the dinner hour. His knock on the door was answered by Jean.

"Come in, we've been expecting you. I'm Jean Pontmercy and this is my wife Francine. Of course you already know Bridgette who arranged this visit. She seems very enthralled by the student debates."

"I'm Enjolras. Your daughter does seem very inquisitive about politics. A little unusual for a girl her age."

Bridgette had just entered the room and was dressed elegantly with an obvious intent to look older and more sophisticated. Enjolras had to admit to himself there was much more charm and beauty to this young lady than pretty eyes and hair. He stood and said, "Mlle. Pontmercy" and appeared to be at a loss for words for one of the few times in his life.

Jean, also an alumnus of the university, opened the discussion, "What do you think of that rascal Gambetta?"

"Probably the best of the Opportunist group," Enjolras replied. "Too flamboyant for my tastes though."

"I believe Jules Ferry has the best future," Jean continued. "President Grevy has very small goals."

Enjolras then praised his favorite, "Georges Clemenceau is a man I could follow. In fact I try to pattern my debates after him. He's great at fencing as well."

"Now, there you have it," Jean countered. "He's too radical. He would overthrow his own mother, if it would advance his cause."

During this time, Bridgette said nothing. She recognized most of the names that were being tossed about, but was content to observe the conversation. Quite naturally she observed Enjolras the majority of the time.

A short time later Francine entered the room with pastries and beverages. After the refreshments Enjolras needed to be on his way home for studying and Bridgette walked him to the front gate. They lingered a few more minutes in the warm September air and then the young man took Bridgette's hand in his and kissed it tenderly and said, "Thank you Mlle. Pontmercy, I really hope we can do this again, often I hope." "Good evening to you M. Enjolras, I hope I, oh, I mean we, can see you again too."

As time went by they did see each other. Except for July and August the discussions became a monthly event. The first year Bridgette's hand was kissed by the debater. The second year Enjolras became a senior and Bridgette entered the university herself. The pair held hands often and took long walks. Before long the kisses flowed as well.

When graduation arrived for Enjolras in May of 1882, he stood fifth in his class overall but first in political science and debating. The influential Jules Ferry was made known of this fact and that he may have a formidable adversary for himself and the Opportunist branch of the government. He was at the time initiating an expansionist policy which was not very popular with his cohorts in high places. He had an idea that may rid himself of a future opponent and also fill an opening for a position which was not destined to have very many volunteers. The week after graduation he arranged for a meeting with Enjolras de Gaulle.

The day of the meeting, Enjolras was kept waiting for 30 minutes and was then ushered into the huge mahogany laden Ferry office.

"Please come in Monsieur. Sorry for the delay, it's been extremely busy."

"M. Ferry, I'm a bit surprised by your invitation."

"I'll get right to the point, Enjolras. Your government keeps close tabs on the top students in several of the best universities. It seems you are the primary choice for a new opportunity overseas."

"Overseas. What exactly does that mean?"

"I'll explain. I'm probably the most radical in a non-radical group of politicians. I believe in the expansion of the French empire. When I say expansion, I mean worldwide. We are founding a large new colony in the Congo Basin and establishing a foothold in Madagascar. I need a man to direct these affairs. Not from behind a desk in Paris but from the African continent itself. I also want a young man, a fresh new face on the scene. A man with resolution and poise. You are my first candidate and the cabinet has agreed to give their support. Well, what do you think?"

"I'll have to give that some thought, M. Ferry. You've caught me off guard to say the least."

"Very well, Enjolras. You have one week to decide. You will leave in three weeks, if you decide in the affirmative."

FAR AWAY PLACES

Following two sleepless nights, Enjolras decided to speak with Bridgette about the offer.

"You want my opinion?" Bridgette began.

"I don't want you to go. If you ever want a future with me, turn it down, please."

"But I'll be paid twice what I could earn here in Paris. And I'll be my own boss. What more could a man ask for?"

Bridgette, slightly miffed, replied "A woman who loves him, that's what!"

"This assignment could take three or four years. I guess that's too long to expect someone to wait."

"That's right Enjolras. It's much too long."

"There may be one solution, Bridgette. But no, that would never work."

"Tell my anyway," she prompted.

"No, your parents......"

"My parents what?" she pleaded.

"All right Bridgette, I'll tell you. Your parents would not like to see their daughter marry and then leave the country."

"If I don't go with you I'm afraid I'll never see you again, but you are right, my love, they would never agree."

"Remember 'Briddy' (a term of endearment he sometimes used) I haven't accepted the position yet."

"Oh, but you will. I know it."

"Perhaps I should just tell him no."

"I can tell you really want this challenge. It sounds like supreme adventure and very romantic as well. I want to be there with you and I think I have a plan that will work."

"Now I am worried," Enjolras said.

"I can almost see the wheels turning in that pretty head of yours."

"Listen to this," she instructed. "Tell your M. Ferry that you will accept his generous offer. We will say nothing to my parents, at least for now. Two days before our departure date we will elope and then arrive at the port city in time for our departure to the African continent. By the way, do your parents know about this?"

"They know about the offer and they also know that I love you. That should be enough for them. They are wrapped up in their own careers you know."

"Good," Bridgette continued.

"I'll write mother and father a lengthy letter explaining everything. They'll be hurt for a while, but they are very understanding. I will assure them my college education will be finished some day."

"I guess you've thought of everything," Enjolras replied.

"I'll inform M. Ferry of my decision tomorrow."

As they embraced for the evenings farewell, he said "I wasn't sure of your long term commitment to me until this evening. I'm glad you didn't disappoint me."

The couple had a somewhat difficult time in maintaining their normal composure during the next two weeks. However, they hid their anticipations and their anxieties well and their magical day was soon upon them. Bridgette packed hurriedly the previous night and was prepared for their trip to Le Havre. They were married in Rouen at a small parish on the outskirts of town. The elderly priest and his wife were the only witnesses to the event as the happy pair would have been unaware of throngs of people, had they been there.

The honeymoon, although sweet and tender, was indeed short as they had to board the ship at Le Havre by the following evening. After all, they reasoned, awaiting them was an ocean voyage where there was ample time to get fully acclimated with married life. Bridgette had arranged for the delivery of her letter to arrive in a timely fashion so as not to worry her parents concerning her whereabouts. The fact that they would not see her again for a long time was another matter.

On the second day at sea the new bride had a complaint.

"My dear Enjolras, I'm quite seasick. My breakfast left me a short time ago. How are you feeling today?"

"Just fine, my little landlubber. You need to stay out on deck more. Breathe plenty of the salt air and enjoy the view."

"Very funny, husband. I hope this doesn't last long or it will be a very difficult trip for me."

Fortunately the malady was only temporary and by the time they reached the Congo their main enemy was the brutal equatorial heat. Within a month Enjolras had set up his headquarters and had hired a national to be in charge of the new facility as he was anxious to be on his way to Madagascar. In recent weeks he had become fascinated with the worlds fourth largest island. By travelling hundreds of miles to the south, they would be distancing themselves from the equator with all its heat and humidity.

This time the trip was much more pleasant and as they neared the Cape of Good Hope Enjolras remarked "Madagascar is huge. Over a quarter of a million square miles in area. Our government will be colonizing and looking for gold and other precious metals in the years ahead. Soon, we hope, the British will recognize the Island as a French protectorate."

"It seems to me you've changed your political persuasions somewhat," Bridgette commented.

"Not really, my dear. I'm biding my time. Right now the Opportunists are firmly entrenched and I'm gaining valuable experience for the future. If I can make a name for myself in the next few years, I'll be ready to make a bold move when the next shift of power occurs."

"I think I understand and my complete support goes without saying. I'll be at your side whatever happens."

Jean and Francine recovered quickly from the initial shock of their daughters departure. They had long since realized that she was the most adventurous of their three children. They both were fond of Enjolras and his potential in the world of government. In addition, a cordial meeting with his parents accomplished much in the soothing of their apprehensions regarding the joining of the dynamic pair.

Charles claimed he suspected something strange was going on with his sister but couldn't prove anything. Suzanne was without a clue as to the plans of her older sister. She was rather oblivious about many subjects, having just recently discovered that boys existed on planet earth.

The ship drifted into the harbor at Diego-Suarez in the early afternoon of a sun drenched mid-September day. The weather and temperature promised to be much more comfortable here with highs' about 80 degrees and overnight lows in the lower sixties. Now that they were south of the equator, still warmer weather was due by December.

Standing side by side on deck Bridgette said to her adoring husband, "Madagascar really is huge. I've been watching the shoreline on and off all morning. We must have reached the southern tip during the night some time."

"That's right, my sweet one," Enjolras agreed. "We'll be living in Diego Suarez at the most northern part of the island. I may be travelling to Tananarive in Central Madagascar next month on business. Of course you'll be staying here in the hotel suite that has been arranged for us."

"That's not fair, darling," she chided.

"It must be! After taking the ship to the mid point of the island I must travel about 75 miles inland. It will be rough in some parts and there is talk of some trouble because of French interest in the Island."

By 1883 the 'trouble' did commence, manifesting itself in the first "Franco Merina" war. The conflict terminated in 1885 with an ambiguous treaty giving France the right to maintain a settlement at Diego-Suarez and a resident at Tananarive. However, the prime minister temporarily managed to avoid the institution of a protectorate.

The happy couple managed to distance themselves from the period of hostilities and, in early 1886, Bridgette had some news for her husband.

"Enjolras, you're going to be a father!"

"Is that right. You know I've been away quite often lately," he teased.

"That's not funny," she said while shaking her small fist at him.

"I'm sorry my dear. Really, this is fantastic news."

"That's better," she continued. "Now I have an order for you, my husband. This child must be born in France. Our four year assignment will be reached this summer and you have accumulated leave time that is due. To be honest I would like to return to Paris in May or June.

"That might be a tall order, dearest, but I'll see what I can do. Who knows, with this recent turmoil behind us, the request should be granted. Lord knows, I do have two or three months owed to me according to my contract."

OUT OF MADAGASCAR

Six weeks went by before they received an answer from their inquiry. Fortunately it was the answer they had hoped and prayed for, and Enjolras burst into the kitchen where his wife was preparing dinner and exclaimed," Here's the letter we have been waiting for and the news is good. We'll be leaving on May 15th and I'll be off until July 15th when I'll receive my new assignment. The letter also makes mention of a monetary award that will be given to me on our return. Apparently M. Ferry was well satisfied with the progress in Africa and here on the island."

"Well, he should be. You give him about 60 hours a week including your travel time," Bridgette remarked.

"By the way, dearest, when are you expecting our new addition to the family?" Enjolras asked.

"Early in October, but mother told me once it's hard to tell, especially for your first."

"Sounds fine to me," said the husband as he went outside to walk and happily ponder his family and his future back in Paris.

By 1890 the British recognized Madagascar as a French protectorate, removing the final barrier to France's control over the island. In 1895 French troops landed at Majunga to quell areas not willing to submit. On September 30, after the only significant battle of the war, Tananarive was occupied and the prime minister was exiled. The queen signed a treaty recognizing the protectorate and was maintained on the throne as a figurehead. The French colonial period thus began and was to extend for the next 50 years.

Some of the lasting fruits of expansionism by France in that period are as follows. The Congo and the Congo basin retained the franc as their permanent form of currency. This was true for Madagascar also. French, as well as the Malagasy dialect, gained official language status in Madagascar. The Congo and other countries of west Africa also enjoy the status of official French speaking nations.

Lest we forget, a daughter was born to Enjolras and Bridgette in early October 7, 1886. On their return they had been welcomed with open arms by both sets of parents. With the extra money gained from the overseers venture they were able to move into a modestly priced home in the university section of the city. The little girl was named Cosette, after Bridgette's grandmother. One more child was born to this couple, a son in November 1890. The family of Enjolras and Bridgette deGaulle was now complete with the birth of their son Charles.

A good name is rather to be chosen than great riches, and loving favour rather than silver and gold.

Prov. 22:1

EPILOGUE

In 1889, exactly one hundred years after the onset of the Revolution, Jean and Francine walked happily along the streets of Paris with their granddaughter. The child was named Cosette, after her great-grandmother, and was almost three. The former Cosette was entering a period of five horrible years at this point in her life while this child was endowed with almost more love and caring than she could assimilate.

They carried a picnic basket amply filled for a nice lunch and afternoon outdoors. As they walked the number of people headed in the same direction increased. Many brought food with them as well. The atmosphere was much like a carnival or some major celebration. Soon they found a pleasant grassy area and settled down.

All eyes were focused toward the same general vicinity. What their eyes beheld was certainly more forgiving than the guillotine of long ago. It was taller than three Bastille's put together. The structure was far more beautiful than any barricade ever built. The reader will have probably guessed by now, they were eating lunch within one hundred yards of the base of the Eiffel Tower.

BIBLIOGRAPHY

Les Misérables - Victor Hugo, 1862 Signet Classic, 1987 Library of Congress catalog card No. 86-62313

Encyclopedia Britannica - 1975, Library of Congress catalog card No. 74-76965, Helen Hemingway Benton, Publisher

National Geographic - July 1989 France Celebrates its Bicentennial

The Holy Scriptures - Authorized King James Version The World Publishing Company, New York, New York 10022

ABOUT THE AUTHOR

As far as I can recall, my father began writing periodically in 1986 at the age of 48. For years he had spoken of writing an auto-biography some day, focusing on his earlier childhood days. From age nine until his marriage, at age 21, he lived with three different sets of aunts and uncles. Although he didn't recall the exact details of his geographical change of residence from north Jersey and alcoholic parents to the suburbs north of Philadelphia, it was apparently out of concern for life and limb. The resulting work was entitled "Say Uncle" and was completed in 1988.

When I, the youngest of four children, moved out of the house to sample life on my own, dad began his hospital volunteer career in the fall of 1987. He continued this work, which consisted of a four-hour shift every Wednesday evening, for four years. By this time he had worked for 35 years, mostly as a buyer, for a major chemical company based in Philadelphia. After keeping a diary of his experiences from week to week, Dad put together a writing which ran the gamut from hilarity to tragedy with everything in between. His duties were that of a pharmacy courier and the diary was titled, "The Halls of St. Mary".

In 1991, Dad wrote a poem for a young girl in our church, which was pastored at that time by my brother. A short time later, Bill put his father on the spot from the pulpit by declaring (in a joval manner) that his father had never written a poem for him. Dad obliged within a month but Bill never once acknowledged that he had received it or whether he liked it. Of course Dad never brought the subject up about the poem. Three months later when Bill moved up to a much larger new church in Florida, he read the poem to approximately 300 people gathered for a farewell dinner honoring his service in the area. Dad was some-what stunned with this development but the attendees loved it and upon learning it was done in the acrostic form spelling out Bill's full name they emitted a small gasp of surprise followed by thunderous applause. Dad now supplies booklets of his poetry captioned, "Inspirational Poetry" to those in the church who are interested or who are just hurting due to recent illness or loss. All his booklets are illustrated with carefully selected pictures from the pages of National Geographic Magazine.

For years Dad's favorite book was "The Tale of Two Cities" with "Great Expectations" a close second. Both of these were, of course, written by Charles Dickens. All this changed dramatically after attending the live musical production of "Les Misérables" in the spring of 1993. Never having read the book, he borrowed my copy, a soft cover abridged version of 560 pages. Becoming totally fascinated with the story he purchased the complete story, over 1400 pages in the soft cover edition. By the fall Dad was convinced the story, although lengthy, was too good to come to an end. The marriage of Marius and Cosette brought visions of new life and new beginnings, not an ending. Why had this not been accomplished by someone in over 130 years, Dad didn't know, but he had to try. Not wishing to mar a classic in any way Dad proceeded in the way he felt Victor Hugo would have wanted the story to progress and put his own wishes for the story aside.

Dad now dreams of visiting the city of Paris and currently spends much of his free time studying the French language. If he does indeed make that trip, I sincerely hope there are no signs of student unrest while he is there. Should a barricade be erected anywhere in Paris, no matter how small, I'm sure he would locate it and make his way there and join the students, with no risk too great.

Kimberly Read-Aroniss

To order additional copies of **The Pontmercy's of Paris**, complete the information below.

Ship to: (please print)

Name _____

Address _____

City, State, Zip _____

Day phone _____

_____ copies of **The Pontmercy's of Paris** @ $12.95 each $ _____

Postage and handling @ $2.50 per book $ _____

PA residents add 6% tax $ _____

Total amount enclosed $ _____

Make checks payable to **W.J. Read**

Send to: W. James Read
2304 Brownsville Road F-15 · Langhorne, PA 19053

To order additional copies of **The Pontmercy's of Paris**, complete the information below.

Ship to: (please print)

Name _____

Address _____

City, State, Zip _____

Day phone _____

_____ copies of **The Pontmercy's of Paris** @ $12.95 each $ _____

Postage and handling @ $2.50 per book $ _____

PA residents add 6% tax $ _____

Total amount enclosed $ _____

Make checks payable to **W.J. Read**

Send to: W. James Read
2304 Brownsville Road F-15 · Langhorne, PA 19053